"*Bad Connection* is a terrific story for anyone who loves supernatural fiction. My daughters are going to be arguing over who gets to read it first."

—RANDY INGERMANSON, winner of two Christy Awards
and author of *Double Vision*

"God does what He wills and cannot be manipulated. This is the sound doctrinal message for Melody Carlson's book *Bad Connection*. Writing about a spiritual gift we rarely see today was risky, but handled so well I would encourage any teen (or their parents) to read this book. I was reminded that we are not to be afraid of God's more unusual gifts, but to allow Him to use them in our lives."

—LISSA HALLS JOHNSON, creator of the Brio Girls
series, coauthor of *A Full House of Growing Pains*

"Bravo to Melody Carlson for creating a wonderful, engaging character who is just like our daughters and the teens in our church. Yet, she's gifted with visions from God. After eighteen years in youth ministry and watching the world present an enticing display of the supernatural, I'm thrilled to see Christian fiction address this issue, letting teens know that greater is He that is in you, than he that is in the world."

—RACHEL HAUCK, author of *Lost in NashVegas*

"*Bad Connection* has it all: suspense, a ripped-from-the-headlines plot, and characters you'd find in any high school. It's a novel I'd definitely recommend to my teenage granddaughters and their friends."

> —PATRICIA H. RUSHFORD, author of the Jennie
> McGrady Mysteries

"Samantha is totally ordinary in an extraordinary way. Not like us yet just like us. Getting to know her is an experience in itself."

> —SARAH ANNE SUMPOLEC, author of the Becoming
> Beka series

"*Beyond Reach* has a story line similar to many popular TV shows today dealing with ordinary people with a 'gift' to see into the future. Yet the main character, Samantha McGregor, has one question: If this is supposed to be a gift from God, why does it seem like a curse? Overall, this page-turning story weaves in suicide, dating relationships, conflicts with parents, and additional issues teens face. As a mom of three teens myself, I'm thankful that these issues can be 'lived out' in a story with a Christian foundation and worldview. Highly recommended!"

> —TRICIA GOYER, author of *Generation NeXt Parenting*
> and *Night Song*

playing
with fire

the secret life of Samantha McGregor
BOOK THREE

playing
with fire

a novel

melody carlson

MULTNOMAH
BOOKS

PLAYING WITH FIRE
PUBLISHED BY MULTNOMAH BOOKS
12265 Oracle Boulevard, Suite 200
Colorado Springs, Colorado 80921
A division of Random House Inc.

Scripture quotations are taken from the King James Version.

The characters and events in this book are fictional, and any resemblance to actual persons or events is coincidental.

ISBN: 978-1-59052-694-1

Library of Congress Cataloging-in-Publication Data
Carlson, Melody.
    Playing with fire : a novel / Melody Carlson.
        p. cm. — (The secret life of Samantha McGregor ; bk. 3)
    Summary: Just before her older brother is due to return from a drug rehabilitation clinic, Sam has a dream about an explosion in a place she believes may be associated with illegal drugs, but she is unsure if this is a vision from God since she is the only person appearing in it. Includes dis-cussion questions, list of key scriptural passages, and suggestions for finding more information about dreams and visions on Web sites.
    ISBN 978-1-59052-694-1
    [1. Christian life—Fiction. 2. Visions—Fiction. 3. Brothers and sisters—Fiction. 4. Drugs—Fiction. 5. Drug abuse—Fiction. 6. High schools—Fiction. 7. Schools—Fiction.] I. Title.
    PZ7.C216637 Pla 2007
    [Fic]—dc22

                                              2007009487

Printed in the United States of America
2007—First Edition

10 9 8 7 6 5 4 3 2 1

Author's Note

I normally don't include a letter in my books, but because The Secret Life of Samantha McGregor series treads on some new territory, I want to make a few things as clear as possible.

First of all, this book is *fiction*—it's simply a story that's meant to entertain and to possibly point out some spiritual truths—but it is *not* a theological study on the proper use of the gifts of the Holy Spirit. While I do believe in the gifts of the Holy Spirit and in God's desire for all of us to do many wonderful things, I also realize that Samantha's gift, her ability to receive dreams and visions from God, is extremely rare. But it does make for a good story!

Second, my hope is that you won't envy Samantha's unusual gift or seek it for yourself, since that would be totally wrong! Don't forget that God is the giver of every good and perfect gift, and *He's* the One who decides who gets what and when it's appropriate to use. If you go around searching for your own gifts, you can put yourself at serious risk. Satan masquerades as an angel of light and delights in tricking those who look for gifts in the wrong places. Don't let that be you.

More than anything, I hope you'll follow Samantha's example by seeking out God and a committed relationship with Him. I hope you'll desire to walk closely with God every day, to make Him your best friend, and to be ready for whatever adventures and gifts He has in store for you. Just make sure they come from God!

And finally, remember that the Bible is our ultimate source for answers to all of life's questions. That's why I've included more Scripture in this series than usual. Also, please check out the resources and discussion questions in the back of this book.

I pray that this fictional journey will draw your heart closer to God and that He will be your lifeline—for today and for always!

Best blessings!

Melody Carlson

A Word from Samantha

The first time it happened, I thought it was pretty weird but kind of cool. The second time it happened, I got a little freaked. The third time it happened, I became seriously scared and had sort of a meltdown. That's when my mom decided to send me to a shrink. She thought I was going crazy. And I thought she was right for a change.

Turns out it was just God. Okay, not just God. Because, believe me, God is way more than just anything. Still, it was hard to explain this weird phenomenon to my mom or the shrink or anyone. It still is. Other than my best friend, Olivia, I don't think most people really get me.

But that's okay, because I know that God gets me. For that reason I try to keep this part of my life under wraps. For the most part anyway.

A Word from the Word...

And ye shall know that I am in the midst of Israel, and that I am the LORD your God, and none else: and my people shall never be ashamed. And it shall come to pass afterward, that I will pour out my spirit upon all flesh; and your sons and your daughters shall prophesy, your old men shall dream dreams, your young men shall see visions: And also upon the servants and upon the handmaids in those days will I pour out my spirit. (Joel 2:27–29, KJV)

My eyes sting from the heat. I blink and rub at them, trying to see what's in front of me, but there's so much smoke I feel blind. And there's a nasty acrid smell that burns my throat as I attempt to breathe. It smells like something very bad is burning, something I shouldn't be inhaling.

As I stumble along, I try to hold my breath. I know that I need to escape this place—*fast!* But then I trip over a wooden crate and fall smack down onto what feels like a filthy cement floor. It's sticky and grimy down here with, I'm guessing, years' worth of crud ingrained into the surface.

Despite the filth, I think maybe I'm safer down here. I recall a fireman, back when I was little, telling our class that the smoke isn't as bad if you stay low. So I continue searching for the exit, crawling on my hands and knees. The air has gotten so thick that it feels like I'm fighting my way through a heavy curtain of murky darkness. I pull the neck of my T-shirt up over my face in an attempt to cover my nose and mouth. I can't see a thing except for the eerie red glow off to my left, and I need to get away from that—it's dangerous, deadly, and evil.

I must keep moving in the opposite direction of the fire. My time is limited, and I need to get out of here—now! Shards of glass cut into my hands and knees as I creep along, and I keep bumping into cardboard boxes and plastic bottles and other sorts of unknown debris cluttering the place. It seems as if someone has been in here knocking things over, throwing things about, creating a huge mess that has become my obstacle course...or perhaps my deathtrap if I don't escape.

I can't give up I tell myself as I continue navigating through my smoky prison. There must be a door some-where. If I got into this place, there has to be a way out. I just wish I knew where it is. I inch my way forward, upright on my knees now, my arms outstretched and flail-ing in front of me. If only I could find a wall to follow. Something that would lead me to a door or a window, anything that could get me out of here.

The heat is almost unbearable now. It feels like the back of my shirt is melting into my skin, like my lungs are about to collapse. And the putrid stench makes me want to vomit. I suddenly wonder if this is what hell would feel like and how anyone could endure such torture. Is that where I am right now—in hell? But why? Why would I be in hell? Why would God allow that?

Finally my hands feel what seems to be a wall. I rise to my feet and quickly use the rough wooden surface to guide me. Splinters pierce my fingers, but that's minor compared to the burning heat and the deadly smell. I work my way along this wall until I reach what I think is a window. It's about three feet from the floor and feels as if a heavy, canvaslike cloth is covering the glass. I tug at the cloth, but it's securely attached by what seem to be nails. Why would someone nail a window covering down?

And then I hear a loud sizzling, crackling noise behind me, back where the fire is increasing by the second. It's a menacing sound...almost demonic, like it wants to devour me, to burn me alive. I pound my fists against the cloth over the window, hoping to loosen this covering and force open the window and—

An earsplitting explosion knocks me off my feet, and I smack into the window.

When I come to my senses, I am lying facedown outside. I don't know how much time has passed, but I'm on pavement that's cool and damp, probably from a recent rain. I can tell that it's night by the darkness and the streetlight several feet away. The ground's wetness is such a welcome relief after the inferno I just escaped and the horrible explosion that I felt certain was going to kill me. But when I slowly roll over onto my back and open my eyes, I see by the glow of the streetlight that what I thought was water is actually my own blood. Bright red blood is flowing everywhere, like a river coming straight out of me. My arms and legs and entire body are sliced and shredded, probably a result of that explosion and my crashing through the window. I become dizzy from looking at the pool of my own blood, or perhaps it's simply from the loss of it. No human can possibly survive so much blood loss without medical assistance. Without help, I will die.

I attempt to scream, but my voice feels small and weak...and the street is completely vacant and quiet, not a car or pedestrian in sight. No one who can possibly come to my rescue.

"Dear God," I sob, "please, please, help me! Help me!" Then I lay my head back and close my eyes, preparing to die, because it won't be long now. It won't be long...

"Samantha!" Someone's shaking me. "Samantha!"

I open my eyes once again, and my mother's face hovers over me with a worried expression. I blink and sit up, realizing that I am safe and in my own bed. I look down at my arms and see that I'm not cut. I'm not bleeding.

"Are you okay?" Mom sits next to me on the bed. "I heard you screaming in your sleep. Sounds like you were having a pretty bad dream."

I'm still trying to catch my breath, to slow down my heart rate.

"Are you okay?" she asks again.

I nod.

My mom's face grows even more troubled now. "Was it one of *those* dreams?"

I know what she means by "those" dreams. I also know that she'd probably rather not hear about it, but I'm still so shaken, so frightened, that I need to talk. "I don't know. All I know is that it was horrid."

"Do you want to tell me about it?"

I frown. "Do you really want to hear?"

She sort of shrugs. "I'm awake... You might as well tell me."

So I describe the dream to her, and her frown lines grow deeper as she listens. "That was awful. Do you think it means anything?"

"I don't know, Mom. I never saw anyone else in the dream. Usually those dreams are warnings for someone else. But it's like I was all alone in this one."

"Surely you don't think something like that could happen to you, do you?"

"I don't know. I mean, I suppose the warning could be for me. And if I ever got into a situation that felt anything like that, well, I'd probably remember this dream and get out of there before things got worse."

Mom sighs, pressing her lips together, and I can tell that I've pushed her beyond her comfort zone.

"The important thing to keep in mind," I tell her, "is that when God gives me prophetic dreams, it's almost always to help someone or to prevent something bad from happening."

She just shakes her head, and I can tell she doesn't get it, doesn't want to get it, and I'm guessing she'd like to go back to bed. "Isn't there a good chance that it was simply a nightmare, Samantha?"

"Maybe…"

"Can you go back to sleep now?" She glances at my alarm clock. "It's not even four yet."

"Yeah, I'll read my Bible for a while." I force a smile for her benefit. "That always makes me feel better."

"Okay." Then she leans over and kisses me on the forehead, something she hasn't done since I was little and she would put me to bed. "Hope you have some better dreams now."

"Me too."

Although I try to appear brave and like I'm perfectly fine, I am haunted by that dream. It felt like the real deal. Yet how can I know for sure? And if it really was from God, what does it mean? Was it meant for me or somebody else?

Before I read my Bible, I get out my special notebook and carefully record all that I can remember from the dream. Just in case this really is a warning of some sort. But to be honest, I seriously hope it's not. The horror of that fire, the smell of that caustic smoke, the idea of being cut up like that and then bleeding to death... Well, it's pretty disturbing stuff.

Sometimes I wonder why God lets me in on these things. My friend Detective Ebony Hamilton says it must be because He can trust me with important things like this, but sometimes I feel more like I'm being tormented. Oh, I try not to think that consciously, because I do feel honored, and I sure don't want God to take this gift away from me. But sometimes, particularly on nights like this when it's hard to go back to sleep after such a vivid dream, I do sort of wonder. Then I remind myself that God's ways are way higher than mine, and even when it doesn't make sense to me, He knows what He's doing. I just need to trust Him.

I also need to pray. And so I do tonight. Usually when I've had a dream or vision like that, I pray for the person involved in the dream, whether I know them by name or simply by remembering the image I saw. The problem with tonight's dream is that there never really seemed to be anyone besides me. So I just pray for the people on my prayer list instead. I go through several of them and finally really lock into praying for my brother, Zach. He's due to come home in less than a week, so I pray that his stint in rehab has changed him for good. I pray that Zach will submit his heart to God and allow Him to direct his life and that God will open lots of exciting new doors for Zach.

After I finish praying, I can't get my older brother out of my head. And it's hard not to get sad when I think about his life. It's even harder to accept the fact that he had a serious methamphetamine addiction. And that it could've sent him to jail for a long time if Ebony hadn't intervened. Ebony used to be my dad's partner on the force, back before he was killed. Consequently, she has a soft spot for our family. And since her brother runs a rehab place up in Washington State, she worked it out so that Zach could go up there for treatment last December.

Originally Zach went in for what was supposed to be sixty days, but then he signed up for an additional thirty. Ebony assured us it was a really good sign that he was serious about recovery. And as I continue to pray for my brother tonight, I feel more hopeful than usual. I try to imagine us being a family again—sharing meals, watching a movie, laughing at old jokes… Oh, I realize it'll never be the same as when Dad was alive, but maybe it will make Mom happier. I can only hope.

The next morning I feel extra tired as Olivia drives us to school, plus I'm still ruminating over last night's dream, trying to discern whether it's from God or just a product of my imagination. As a result, I'm probably quieter than usual.

"You okay, Sam?" My best friend peers curiously at me after parking her car in the school lot.

"I guess…" Then since Olivia is my only real confidante (well, besides Ebony, but that's different), I tell her about my dream.

"That's so creepy."

"I know."

"Do you think it was from God?"

I shrug. "I don't really know. I mean, I haven't been focusing on any new cases with Ebony, not since solving the Peter Clark one a couple of weeks ago. And I haven't heard anything in the news. Plus there was no one in the dream, I mean, besides me... I just don't know for sure."

"Well, God knows," says Olivia.

"Yeah. I'm just trying to trust Him with this. I figure if it's important, He'll let me know."

She sort of laughs. "I'm sure He will, Sam."

We notice Garrett Pierson slowly coming our way. Olivia waves, and we pause on the steps by the front entrance to wait for him. "Hey, Garrett," I say.

"How's it going?" asks Olivia.

As usual, Garrett's first reaction (looking down at his shoes) reveals just how insecure this guy still is, but then he sort of recovers and actually looks directly at us. "Okay, I guess."

"Hey, I like your shirt." Olivia points at what I'm guessing is another new item of clothing. His foster mom seems to have a pretty good sense of style and has been getting some things to update his previously pathetic wardrobe. Even his shaggy brown hair looks neater these days, and his new glasses have dark frames that actually look sort of cool.

"Yeah," I agree, "that's a good color on you, Garrett."

He thanks us, then grins at me. "Ready for the chem test today, Sam?"

I let out a groan as I remember that it's Friday, test day as always. "Yeah, right. Thanks for reminding me." Garrett's my lab partner, and I depend on him a lot, but when it comes to tests, I'm on my own.

"Don't worry," he assures me. "You'll do fine. You just need more confidence."

I nod as I consider the irony of his advice. Garrett, the academic geek, telling me that I need more confidence. Go figure. "Confidence is good, but a scientific brain wouldn't hurt much either."

"Hey, Olivia," Cameron says as he comes over to join us. Cameron is the leader of a band called Stewed Oysters that Olivia recently began singing vocals with. "You ready for tonight's gig?"

She nods, but she has a look of uncertainty in her eyes. This has to do with the fact that they're playing for Amanda Brow's sweet-sixteen party, and you can never be too sure with those things. Anyway, Olivia's worried it could turn out to be a wild drinking party, which she has no desire to be involved in. I already promised to go with her, and if it gets raunchy, we'll just leave. "I think so," she tells him.

"Cool." Cameron gives her one of those smiles that tells me he's still wishing she'd go out with him. But I happen to know it's a lost cause since Olivia refuses to date a guy who's not a Christian. Then he waves and heads over to where Jack McAllister is smoking a cigarette and waiting for him with his usual grim, bad-boy look.

"Is Jack still treating you like you've got cooties?" asks Garrett.

Olivia pushes a strand of blond hair behind her ear and sighs. "Yeah. But I've noticed he treats a lot of people like that. He's not exactly Mr. Congeniality, if you know what I mean."

"It's because he's a doper," Garrett says in a nonchalant tone. "They're always in a bad mood."

I'm surprised at this coming from Garrett. He's usually not that judgmental. "Do you know for a fact that he uses?" I quietly ask Garrett as the three of us line up to go through security. Brighton High was one of the last schools in the Portland metro area to get a system, but it's supposed to be one of the best.

"Everyone knows that, Sam." He tosses his back-pack into a scanner tray, then walks through the metal-detector gates.

I consider this as I make my way through the check station. Jack McAllister has been on my prayer list ever since Olivia auditioned with the band last month. At the time I thought he might've been a potential suicide case, but after I figured out that it was Garrett who was actually at risk for taking his own life, I sort of forgot about Jack. I pray for him at times but never with much clarity. Still, it should be obvious that Jack is the kind of guy who needs to have people praying for him. Especially if he's seriously into drugs.

I know for a fact, thanks to my brother's struggles, that drugs can unravel a life in a very short time. But I suppose it's one of those things I just don't like to think about much. Maybe it's my personal form of denial. I'm starting to wonder just how prevalent drugs are in the lives of my classmates. Maybe it's something I should be a little more concerned about.

Especially considering my latest dream. After writing down all my notes last night, I felt fairly certain that what-ever was going on in that horrible place that had turned into an inferno was related to drugs. Whether it was the nasty smell of the smoke, the general filth, the boxes and junk all over the floor, or the canvas covering nailed on the window, I concluded that something illegal was going on in there. Now I have to wonder if it's related to Jack McAllister too.

TWO

So how'd you fare?" Garrett asks as we exit chemistry class.

I roll my eyes, then restrain myself from wiping imaginary sweat from my brow. "I guess I'll find out on Monday."

"Don't worry. I'm sure you at least pulled a C or maybe a D."

"Great." I try not to consider what this will do to my GPA.

"When it looked like you were stuck, I thought about slipping you some of the answers."

I turn and stare at my lab partner. "Thanks anyway, Garrett, but I do *not* cheat."

He laughs. "Too bad. I'm guessing that at least half the class does."

Now this actually shocks me. *"Seriously?"*

He just shrugs. "Yeah. If you hadn't been so busy trying to come up with the right answers, you'd have seen them too." Then he goes into some detail about how Ryan Grant was slipping Ashley Summers the answers under the lab table.

"Doesn't Dynell notice it?"

"Apparently not."

"Do *you* ever cheat?" I ask.

He tilts his chin up. "*I* don't need to."

I make a face at him. "You know, for a guy who has kept such a low profile all these years, you sure seem to know a lot about what other people are doing."

"Yeah, well, a guy like me has time to pay attention."

I lower my voice. "You know what you said about Jack McAllister this morning? Is that really true, or are you just making some wide, sweeping assumptions?"

"I can see the signs."

"What signs?" Now I actually know what a lot of the signs are since I've seen them in my brother, but I'm curious whether Garrett really knows what he's talking about or not. Sometimes this guy boggles my mind.

"You know, those sores that look like zits but probably aren't, his generally checked-out or irritable attitude, the kids he hangs with, the way he takes off to be alone so much… So what do *you* think he's doing when he's hiding out, Sam? Praying or meditating?"

"I know you're probably right," I admit as we pause in front of the hallway that leads to the social-science department. "But I guess I just like to give people the benefit of the doubt. I don't like to make accusations."

Garrett frowns like I've hit a sore spot now. "I've gotta respect that you don't do that, Sam. Guess I can be a jerk sometimes."

"I wasn't pointing a finger," I say quickly. "It's just the way I try to be."

"Yeah, but what about me?" he says. "You came to the conclusion that I was the one writing to the suicide Web site. How do you explain that little *assumption*?"

"I guess it's a fine line I have to walk," I tell him. "Sort of a God-thing or spiritual discernment or something that's hard to explain to a nonbeliever. But at least it worked out for the best, don't you think?"

Now he looks frustrated and slightly confused, and I feel bad that I don't have more time to help him understand what I'm trying to say. Despite his I-don't-care attitude, I get the feeling that Garrett really is hungry to learn more about God and faith. And both Olivia and I have been trying to help him. "I gotta go to class right now, but how about if you come with Olivia and me tonight?"

He makes a funny face. "You mean to that sweet-sixteen party?"

I nod. "Yeah, we'll be groupies with the band."

"Guess that could be interesting."

"Okay then. We'll pick you up around seven."

"You sure Conrad won't be jealous?"

"You know they have that away game tonight."

"Why aren't you going?" he asks as the warning bell rings.

"It's like a hundred miles away."

He laughs. "In other words, you're like me—car-less."

I roll my eyes, then make a dash for my U.S. History class. I'm guessing Garrett's going to be late for his class now. Not that anyone will give him a bad time. I mean, sheesh, the guy's got at least a four point GPA and never gives anyone a bit of trouble. Why would they care?

I still find it hard to believe that he was thinking of ending his life less than a month ago. And I'm so glad he didn't. So glad that God used me to intervene with him. And it's been interesting getting to know him better since then. He's been going to counseling, dealing with his depression, and trying to figure out whether he's really gay or not. It turns out that his dad was the one who planted that idea in his head in the first place. His dad, the big "macho" man, was always putting Garrett down because he liked books better than sports. And when Garrett was too shy to go out with girls, his dad started teasing him and calling him "Fairy Boy" and even worse names. Garrett told me that his dad had been emotionally abusive to his mother too, and she finally had enough.

"She found another guy," Garrett confessed to me about a week ago. "Apparently that guy treated her right. She ran off with him when I was thirteen, far enough away that Dad couldn't go after her. It's been just Dad and me since then. And his disposition didn't improve a bit after she left."

Fortunately, Garrett is in a good foster home now. I know that some people might think "good foster home" sounds like an oxymoron, but it turns out there really are some good foster parents out there. Garrett's happen to go to Ebony's church, and she knew they were great with teens.

Garrett seems to be pretty much okay with them too, although he has complained about how they have to pray before every meal and how they have "Bible verses plastered all over the walls like it's a church or something." I reminded him that there were worse things in life, and he didn't argue.

At the end of the day, I tell Olivia about inviting Garrett to join us, and she's fine with it. "He can keep me company while I make sure you're okay tonight," I say as we walk to her car. "So are you still feeling uneasy about it?"

"I'm just not sure," she says as she digs for her keys. "Maybe a little…"

"Then maybe you shouldn't go."

"I've considered backing out, but I've been really praying about it, and I think my fear has more to do with my comfort zone. I don't get the impression that God is telling me to back out."

"Then let's go and see what happens."

"And if it goes south, we can at least count on Garrett to help us get out of there."

I laugh as I imagine the three of us making a getaway. "Yeah, what a scene that would be, huh?"

"Well, from what I've heard around school, there will probably be alcohol at the party."

"I guess I'd be surprised if there wasn't."

Olivia nods as she starts her car. "Yeah, I can't believe how many kids actually drink, I mean, even at school. Did you see Kevin Renner today?"

"No, but I know what you're talking about."

"He was totally wasted. Someone said he'd been sipping straight vodka from his water bottle all day. He actually passed out in my lit class."

"That's so sad."

"Mrs. Kimball thought he was having a *little nap*," says Olivia.

"Teachers can be so oblivious."

"Maybe it's a survival skill."

"I know alcohol's a problem, but I've been wondering how many kids at our school do serious drugs as well."

"Well, obviously you've always got your losers doing drugs.

But those numbers can't be nearly as high as for those who drink. Do you think?"

I get sort of quiet now, thinking about my brother and how some people probably consider him a loser, and that makes me sad. I think he just got mixed up, and I'm sure he's going to be past that now.

"Oh, I'm sorry," Olivia says suddenly. "I just realized that you're probably thinking about Zach. I wasn't trying to say that he's a loser, Sam. He's not. Really. Zach is cool."

"It's okay. I happen to agree that doing drugs can turn anyone into a loser. But I also know that some people who are just regular, nice people—like Zach—get caught up in drugs. They were never losers before. They just got messed up, you know?"

"I know."

"I've been thinking about Jack McAllister, trying to remember what he was like in middle school. Before he got into drugs. Wasn't he pretty quiet back then?"

"Yeah. He was pretty shy too. Nothing like the loud-mouth he is now."

"He really changed."

Olivia frowns. "So you think he's into drugs?"

"Don't you?"

"I guess…"

"Garrett and I were talking about that whole thing. He helped me realize it's probably true. I mean, he's right. All the signs are there. What else could it be?"

Olivia sighs loudly. "Man, if you're right…well, it makes it even harder for me, being in a band where I'm pretty sure someone's using. Maybe I should just quit right now, Sam."

"Or just pray about it. Remember how Jesus hung with a whole lot of sinners and how the Pharisees were always ragging Him about it? But Jesus told them that those were the kind of people He came to help. He said it was the sick who needed a doctor. So you can't just give up on someone like Jack McAllister."

"But it's not like I'm going to go out back and smoke dope with him either."

"Duh." I laugh as I imagine sweet Olivia out in some back alley smoking crack with Jack McAllister. Talk about your impossible scenario.

"Sometimes it feels like a tightrope walk, huh?"

I nod. "Guess those are the times we need to be sure we're holding on to God's hand."

She smiles. "You got that right."

We agree to be praying about the outcome of this evening, and I feel particularly drawn to pray for Jack and Garrett. I just have a strong feeling that God is at work in both of their lives. Okay, I'll admit that you can't really tell by looking at either of them, but God does work in some mysterious ways.

I'm absently flipping through the channels in the family room when I notice my mom coming downstairs with her denim jacket slung over one arm. Her makeup looks fresh, and she has on her "cool" jeans, a new top, and some dangly beaded earrings. "Are you going out tonight?"

"Yes. Paula's picking me up in a few minutes."

I can't help but frown at this news. It seems whenever Mom and Paula go out, which has turned out to be at least once a week, it always involves drinking—too much drinking. Oh, Mom hasn't gotten totally hammered like she did that first night when she broke the ginger-jar lamp, but still it's a concern. A big concern.

Mom gives me a stiff smile. "It's just girls' night out, Sam."

"I know…but it worries me."

She gives me a placating pat on the back. "Remember, sweetie, I'm the mom here. You're the teenager. Don't obsess."

"Who's driving?"

She straightens up and gives me a warning look. "Paula."

"Well, what if she has too much to drink?"

"Paula is very careful. She knows when enough is enough. And besides, if I had any concerns, I'd simply call a cab. You don't need to worry." Then she turns and walks away. What can I say?

Shortly after Mom leaves with Paula, Olivia arrives, and I try not to laugh at her weird outfit—a lacy and somewhat fluffy white dress, topped with a black leather motorcycle vest and accented with short black boots. It's straight out of the eighties and totally unlike her. Even her hair is pulled high on her head in a wild bun/ponytail with blond strands sticking out in all directions.

"You look great," I tell her.

She just laughs as she checks her image in the big mirror by our front door. "I look ridiculous," she says. "But it's all about the music." Then she points at me. "*You* look great."

I shrug as I study my rather ordinary image, compared to hers anyway. My shoulder-length, curly brown hair is actually being pretty cooperative tonight. Not too frizzy.

My hazel eyes look almost brown thanks to the black turtleneck I'm wearing. And I must admit that my silver dangly earrings look pretty cool. I thank her for the compliment, then we get in her car and head over to Garrett's to pick him up.

"I'm so glad you two are coming along tonight," Olivia says as she drives across town. "I really appreciate the moral support."

"I think it'll be interesting," Garrett says in a slightly sly tone. "I've never been to a sweet-sixteen party before."

"Ugh," says Olivia. "I never wanted to have one myself. I think they're a waste of time and money."

"I think it's just a way for parents to show off," I say. But then I check myself since that sounds pretty judgmental. "Although this could be different. You never know."

Garrett laughs. "Then you don't know Amanda Brow, do you?"

"And you do?" I challenge him.

"Well, not personally, but I know *about* her."

"What do you know about her?"

"She's a pretty wild girl," he tells us. "And she wants her party to be the hot topic at school next week."

"Oh, Garrett," teases Olivia, "you're such a gossip."

"Just saying what I heard."

Amanda Brow's house is in a pretty upscale neighborhood. Almost as nice as Olivia's. There are very few cars when we arrive, and after Olivia parks in front, Amanda's mother comes over and tells her to park in the back. "The caterers and workers are parking back here," she says, as if we're the cleanup crew. I'm tempted to point out that Olivia is lead singer for the band and almost famous, but I control myself as Olivia wedges her car back into an alleylike driveway that I'm sure is for their hired help. Like, whatever!

Then as we're walking to the front of the house, Amanda's mother waves us toward the back entrance. And she continues to tell other people where to park, where to take things, and what to do. I think maybe she was an army general before she married Amanda's dad, who I happen to know is big time into real estate.

The rest of the band is already there and partially set up. Cameron has on what looks like a fifties sports coat, and his sandy hair is slicked back in a way that makes him look older and kind of cool, in a slightly geekish way. The other guys are dressed similarly, except for Jack, who looks the same as always. Olivia joins them and does her part in the setup, and Garrett and I park ourselves in a couple of chairs that we managed to scavenge from the dining room. Hopefully, Amanda's mother won't freak. She seems to have her hands full getting everyone into place, acting like this is actually a post–Oscar Awards party. It officially begins at seven thirty, and while a number of Amanda's parents' friends are here, I have a feeling most of the younger guests won't be here any sooner than eight, and I haven't seen a sign of Amanda anywhere.

"You kids can start playing." Mrs. Brow glances at her watch.

"But no one's here," points out Cameron.

She scowls. "*My* friends are here. And I hired you to play from seven until midnight. So play."

Cameron gives her a fake-looking smile, then turns

to his band. "Okay, *kids,* let's play some tunes for the old folks."

Dirk makes a little joke, and Jack lets loose with a foul word that Mrs. Brow doesn't hear, but then the band starts to play. Just jamming sort of playing, but it sounds pretty good, and although the old folks seem oblivious, at least Garrett and I are enjoying it. This goes on for about an hour with only a handful of younger guests trickling in, and they don't look terribly comfortable. Plus, Amanda hasn't made an appearance yet.

"Let's take a break," says Cameron. But they've barely stopped playing and gotten sodas from the kitchen when Mrs. Brow is on their case to start playing again.

It's about eight thirty when a large crowd of kids finally bursts into the house with Amanda in their midst. I can tell Amanda's parents are miffed at their daughter, but they do a pretty good job of concealing it as they bring out a huge cake, and the band plays a rousing chorus of "Happy Birthday to You." The house gets louder and fuller, and after a while Amanda's parents and their older friends sort of disappear. I'm not sure if they've left the residence completely or simply retreated to a different room. But the party definitely begins to get wilder. And it's obvious that alcohol has been sneaked into the house and equally obvious that some of the kids are overdoing it.

I can tell by Olivia's expression that she's not appreciating this chaotic atmosphere, but she's being a good sport and singing well, and some of the guests actually seem to be enjoying the music. But when the band takes its second break a little past ten thirty, Olivia takes Garrett and me aside.

"I don't feel good about this," she tells us. "Kids are getting seriously drunk."

"That's not all." Garrett nods at a particularly rowdy group of partyers clustered on the patio by the pool. "I heard a guy in the kitchen bragging about how he snagged a bunch of ecstasy before coming here. He's handing it out to girls like it's candy."

"No way!" Olivia's blue eyes get big. "And do they really think it's candy?"

He shakes his head. "Only if they're totally stupid... or drunk."

"I don't like this either." I glance over my shoulder to where a girl has just been tossed into the pool. Now I'm sure the pool is heated, but it's like sixty degrees out and not exactly swimming weather.

"I'll tell Cameron that I'm leaving," says Olivia. "They can have my share of tonight's earnings."

The guys in the band are just returning from their break and look pretty ticked at Olivia as she explains the situation. But she stands her ground, and finally Cameron acts like he gets it and waves her away.

"That's what you get for asking little Miss Goody-Goody to sing in the band," Jack says in a fairly loud voice.

"Hey, you should be happy," Garrett tells him. "Now you can take over vocals and put an end to this party."

Jack glares at Garrett, and for one very uncomfortable moment, I think maybe Jack is going to punch my lab partner. I grab Garrett by the arm. "Let's get outta here." I tug him toward the back door.

But when we get back to Olivia's car, we realize that it's totally blocked in by the other cars. "There's no way I can get out of here," she says. We look at the cars wedged in all around us and see that it's hopeless.

"If the caterers could move their rig," says Garrett, pointing at the white van parked next to the edge of the driveway, "you could probably slip out on that side if you were careful."

"Yeah," says Olivia. "I think you're right. I'll go ask them now."

Garrett and I stay outside and wait by the car, but when a couple of guys get into a fight over a girl just a few feet away from us, we actually step in and make a feeble attempt to break it up. Fortunately, it seems like one of the guys is not in a serious fighting mood, not to mention he's pretty drunk, and he appears relieved to be interrupted.

"You need to go home and sleep it off," Garrett tells him. Then the feistier guy starts swearing at Garrett and asking him if he wants to fight.

"No, he doesn't want to fight," I tell the guy. "See ya around." Then I grab Garrett by the arm again, tugging him off to where Olivia is finally emerging from the house.

"The caterer will be out in a few minutes," she announces. "She says she just needs to pack up some of her stuff and get out of there. Man, that party's getting totally crazy. I can't believe Amanda's parents don't care. How can they possibly not hear all this noise?"

"Because they're not home," Garrett informs us.

"How do you know?" I ask.

"I saw their car leaving awhile ago. Didn't you notice, Sam?"

"Obviously not, but I'm glad to know you don't miss a thing."

"Let's wait in the car," Olivia says in a tired voice. "I'll put in a CD, and we can just chill for a while."

So we get into her car, and she slips in a Jennifer Knapp CD. We lean back and listen while we wait for the caterer to move her van.

"It's been almost a half hour," I complain to Olivia. "Maybe you should go see if she forgot about—" In that same instant, a bright light shines in the car window, and someone is knocking loudly on the driver's side. Olivia opens the window a crack, and a loud male voice tells us to get out of the car.

"It's a cop!" says Garrett.

I squint to see through the glaring light and realize that once again Garrett is absolutely right. It is a cop. In fact, it's two cops. And not ones I recognize.

"You kids have some drugs in there?" asks one.

"No, of course not," exclaims Olivia.

"That's not what we were told," says the cop. "Now, everyone, get out slowly and put your hands on top of the car."

As we're doing this, the other cop shines a flashlight around the interior of the car. Then he bends down and reaches into the backseat and removes something from the floor, but I can't see what it is. I assume it's a soda cup or something, although Olivia usually keeps her car pretty tidy.

"What are they looking for?" Olivia whispers to me in a quavery voice.

"They probably think we've been drinking," I say. "We can easily prove that we haven't."

Then the cop removes Olivia's and my bags and Garrett's backpack and sets them on the hood. He continues his senseless search, then finally says something to the cop who is watching us, something we can't hear. And before we know what's happening, we are being arrested and frisked and loaded into a patrol car.

"How can they just arrest us like that?" asks Garrett. "Without any evidence or anything?"

"I don't know," I admit.

"Look." Olivia points toward her car, where one of the cops is holding up something, showing it to the other cop. "What's that in his hand?"

"It looks like a Ziploc bag," I say. "Probably just some garbage you left in your car."

"I do not leave garbage in my car. Did you guys leave something there?"

"Not me." Garrett shakes his head.

"I didn't either," I tell her. "Don't worry. It's probably nothing."

"Yeah," says Garrett. "It looks empty."

As it turns out, we are informed at the police station that the bag wasn't completely empty. And unfortunately for Olivia and Garrett and me, they are convinced that it has trace amounts of methamphetamines in it, so it's being tested in the lab, and we now have a lot of explaining to do.

t seems a little ironic that you were the one who was
worried about *me* getting into trouble tonight," Mom
says as she drives away from the police station at a little
past midnight. I've already explained to her what happened,
right after I told the whole story to Eric Reinhart, the cop
who took my statement, a guy I already know from working with Ebony. He knows that I work for the police and
that I have a "special gift." So how embarrassing was
that? But at least he seemed to understand. He told me
not to worry about it, that it'd work itself out. That's a
whole lot more than I can say for my mom, who seems
intent on torturing me a little bit longer.

"I told you that *wasn't* our bag," I say for like the hun-
dredth time.

She sort of laughs. "Well, I'm fairly certain it wasn't *yours,*
Samantha. But how do you know about your friends? Not
that I can imagine Olivia being into that sort of thing. But
what about that Garrett character? We don't know much
about him, and he did try to kill himself last month. That
instability might be symptomatic of an addiction problem."

"I seriously don't think Garrett is a user." I fold my arms
across my chest and stare out the passenger window.

Why is my mom being like this? I mean, sure, she didn't like having to come to the police station to pick me up, but it's not like this whole thing was my fault either. So why does she start assuming one of us really is guilty? Olivia admitted to everyone that she'd forgotten to lock her doors tonight. Probably the result of bossy Mrs. Brow telling her to move her car after she'd parked it once. It's entirely possible that someone actually got into the backseat of Olivia's car, did some drugs back there, then left their stupid Ziploc bag behind. Or maybe someone wanted to frame us and tossed in a piece of evidence and then told the cops.

Otherwise, why would the cops come looking for us? Sure, they were breaking up the party, probably because it was so loud, and I'm guessing the neighbors complained. Consequently, quite a few kids (the ones who didn't make it out in time) got arrested for "minor in possession" and other alcohol-related charges. But what made the police head for Olivia's car? All these questions are tumbling through my head, and it doesn't help matters to have my mom pointing the finger at Garrett just now. I'm mad enough not to talk to her. For her to try to link his suicide attempt to a drug-addiction problem is just plain mean.

Seriously, I don't think Garrett uses anything, but I don't know this for an absolute fact. And it's possible that a person who has been through as much as Garrett might turn to a substance to relieve his pain, to sort of self-medicate, but I don't think that's the case with him. It just doesn't ring true. He seems too smart to get messed up with something like meth.

Then I think of Zach. He was smart too. Before he started dabbling in drugs, he was at the top of his class. Suddenly I'm thinking that maybe I don't have the slightest clue about any of this crud. I am in way over my head. Mostly I want to forget the whole thing. I want to go to bed, then wake up and find out this whole evening was just another bad dream. What does any of this really have to do with me anyway? I didn't have anything to do with that stupid Ziploc bag, and I don't have anything to do with drugs. Then I remember last night's dream. I remember the heat of that fire and the stench of the smoke and my conclusion that it was somehow drug related. What was that all about? I sense it was from God, but why? And suddenly I wonder about Garrett. He was the one in the backseat. It's not like I was watching him. Maybe God knows that Garrett has a problem...maybe my dream was a warning for Garrett.

And yet, he seemed as shocked as we were by the discovery of that bag. On the other hand, Garrett is wicked smart. And he's a good actor too. He had me totally fooled about being suicidal. And then he nearly jumped off that bridge. Maybe Mom is right about him. Maybe I'm clueless. Even so, I won't give in to her about this tonight. I will remain loyal to my friend.

"Sorry I ruined your evening," I say as I get out of the car. I'm trying to sound sincere, but I have a feeling she doesn't hear it like that.

"Well, I'm going to leave it to you to sort this thing out," she says as she unlocks the door. "I'm guessing that between Ebony and your other police friends, it should be no problem."

I want to say "duh," but that would sound pretty disrespectful. Still, it's better than what I'm thinking of saying, like, *Don't I always sort out my own life, Mom?* Or like, *Since when have you been very involved in my life anyway?* But I don't say these spiteful things. I just go to my room and restrain myself from slamming the door. Then I pray for God to change my heart.

The next morning Olivia picks me up, according to the plan we made last night. We both decided that we're not going to take this crud without a fight.

"So your dad got your car back with no problems?" I ask as I climb in.

"Sometimes it helps being the city attorney."

"Meaning he pulled some strings?"

"I wouldn't say that. But he does know his way around the legal system. He knows how to play the game."

"I still can't believe what happened last night," I say as she drives us to the police station. Our plan is to talk to Ebony this morning. I called earlier to set it up. Fortunately, she was at the station and had already heard about our little ordeal.

"My mom keeps saying that it was probably just a careless, random sort of thing, and we should just forget all about it, but my dad's not so sure. He thinks it was a setup. But then, of course, he thinks like a lawyer."

"But if it was a setup, who would've done it?"

"Well, I don't like to make accusations, but Jack McAllister seems a fairly obvious suspect."

"Yeah, I'd thought of him too."

"The band had a couple of breaks last night, and like usual, Jack took off by himself, so who knows what he was up to. Usually I assume he's just grabbing a cigarette, but after what Garrett said, well, I'm thinking drugs were probably more likely."

"And Jack really seems to have it out for you. Plus he was ticked at Garrett last night."

"My dad is a little suspicious of Garrett too."

"Really?"

"I told him he was wrong, but he says that if Garrett was in the backseat, he would be the most likely suspect."

"My mom thought the same thing."

"What do you think, Sam?"

"I hate to say it, but I guess we can't deny the possibility that he might have left it there."

"But Garrett just doesn't seem like the type…"

"What *is* the type, Olivia?" I hear the irritation in my voice and wish I could retract it. Still, I get tired of people assuming that anyone who uses is a messed-up, burned-out psychopath. It's just not fair, not true, and I feel defensive of Zach.

"I know…I know…there isn't really *a type.* And I'm not going to head down the 'loser' road again, Sam. It's just that Garrett has been pretty vocal against drugs, and he seems serious about school… It just doesn't make sense."

"But remember how Garrett made that joke about Jack being a woman-hater, saying it was probably because Jack was gay? If you think about it, it could've been an act, like a smoke screen for Garrett's own sexual orientation, to throw us off his trail, you know?" Okay, now I'm playing devil's advocate by pointing the finger at my friend. But a good detective explores all the possibilities.

"But we don't even know for sure that Garrett is gay."

I push a strand of curly hair away from my eye and let out a big sigh. "You know, the more I think about all this, nothing makes much sense. Maybe we should do whatever it takes to get this thing cleared up and then just forget all about it."

"Maybe..." Then we're back at the police station.

"Do you realize we were here less than twelve hours ago?" I point out as I notice the big clock above the receptionist's desk.

"At least we didn't have to spend the night."

I wave at the receptionist, who recognizes me, then lead Olivia back to Ebony's office. And, okay, I know I'm totally innocent of that stupid meth accusation, but I still feel sort of guilty as we walk down the hall.

"Ebony knows we're coming, right?" asks Olivia.

I nod as I knock on the partially opened door.

"Hi, girls," Ebony calls out. "Come on in."

We go in, sit down, and take turns pouring out our story. She asks us some routine questions, looks over our files, which she's obviously already gone through, then tells us that we should have nothing to worry about. "Possession of a controlled substance is a serious charge, but chances are it will be dropped by Monday."

"That's what my dad said too," admits Olivia.

"But I just wanted to be sure," I tell her. "I mean, it's kind of embarrassing being mixed up in all this, especially since I'm sort of working with you now." I've already told Olivia, in confidence, about being on retainer with the Brighton Police Department. Besides my mom, Olivia's the only one outside of the department who knows about this.

Ebony smiles, and I'm reminded of how pretty she is. Her white teeth almost seem to sparkle against her bronze-colored skin. "I don't think anyone here really believed you were directly involved in last night's bust, Samantha."

I let out a little sigh of relief.

Then she studies me. "But what about Garrett? Where does he fit into all this?"

Both Olivia and I attest to our belief in his innocence. But even as I defend Garrett, I have a tiny sliver of doubt. I mean, how can we be absolutely certain?

"I'm surprised you didn't invite him to join you here today." Ebony closes the files and stacks them together.

"I know…," I say with regret. "I thought about that on the way over, but Olivia and I sort of put this plan together last night. Garrett was still answering questions, and we didn't see him before we went home."

"I like Garrett, and his foster family seems very pleased with how he's doing, but even so, there's a real possibility he might be responsible for the evidence found in Olivia's car. It wouldn't be the first time a kid who has been emotionally abused sought an escape through illegal drugs."

"I've considered that possibility too," I admit, "but I just don't think that's the case."

"Do you think he'd be willing to have a drug test?"

"We could call and ask him," I suggest.

"If he gets it done today, it could be used as evidence in his defense and might get his charges dropped."

"I'll call him right now." Olivia excuses herself and opens her cell phone.

After she's gone, Ebony asks how I'm doing, and I take the opportunity to tell her about my latest dream as well as my sudden interest and concern over drug use in our area.

"Well, you should be concerned." Ebony's brow creases in frustration. "*Everyone* should be concerned. The number of addicts in our town is on the rise. The crime rate is on the rise. And I'd estimate that about ninety percent of our crime incidents are drug related. It's costing our community more than anyone can begin to imagine. And yet the average citizens just seem to ignore it, as if it'll simply go away, like a twenty-four-hour flu or a seven-day cold. But the reality is, this problem is more like an epidemic, and before it's over, many people will be affected by it."

I nod. "Yeah, I know that personally."

"How is Zach?" She leans over with real interest.

"Last time I talked to him, a few days ago, he sounded really good. Just like the old Zach."

"Doesn't he come home soon?"

"Next Thursday."

"That's wonderful, Samantha. But I hope you realize that just because he has completed a ninety-day treatment program, it doesn't mean he's cured."

I frown. "What do you mean?"

"He'll need to continue treatment. He'll need to keep going to rehab meetings and to meet with his mentor. It'll be up to him to work his recovery program on the outside now. The final outcome is in Zach's hands."

"Oh…" Now, to be honest, I hadn't considered any of this, and I feel a little disappointed. I guess I just really wanted to return to *life as normal*—the way it was before Zach ever got involved with drugs.

"The fact is that a meth addict isn't considered 'recovered' until he's been clean for at least two years."

I blink. "Two years?"

She nods. "That's what my brother has told me."

"He should know."

"And I'm going to tell you something else that's hard to hear, Samantha…" She pauses as if considering whether to continue or not.

"Yes?"

"Well, in all likelihood, Zach will use again."

I feel like I've just been punched in the stomach.

"It's tough to hear, but it's the truth. Following a recovery program, most addicts fall off the wagon and use again. But according to my brother, a lot of them get so disgusted at themselves for using that it becomes a reminder that they really want to be clean."

"But they don't all do this, right?"

"No. There are those who get it the first time." She frowns. "But they are a minority, Samantha."

"Maybe Zach will be in that minority. I mean, he's a smart kid. He was raised in a good home. He should be able to figure this out, don't you think?"

She sort of smiles. "Well, let's hope so. But don't be too disappointed if that's not the case, okay?"

I say, "Okay," but I'm thinking, *No way. Zach won't go back to that crud. He's smarter than that.*

"I just talked to Garrett," Olivia announces as she comes back into the office. "He's willing to do a drug test." Then she smirks. "Okay, he's not exactly thrilled with the idea, and he thinks it's totally unfair and that it might somehow infringe on his constitutional rights. But I convinced him that doing this *today* could save him some trouble later."

"Great," says Ebony. "I'll have Claudia set it up with him for this afternoon."

"Do we need to be tested too?" I ask, still feeling bummed about what Ebony just told me.

Ebony shrugs. "It's up to you. But it couldn't hurt."

And so, just to be safe, Olivia and I both agree to be tested. Ebony goes out with us and introduces us to a large, no-nonsense woman named Claudia that I've seen before. This woman looks like she could play the part of a prison guard for a Nazi internment camp. With a grim expression, she hands us our plastic cups, then escorts us to the ladies' room, where she makes certain that we "make our deposits without cheating." It's all very humiliating, and I feel like a criminal as I hand my now-filled container back to Claudia.

"Are you going to supervise Garrett too?"

She gives me a stern look. "No, we have a male clerk who will take care of that."

"Gee, that was fun," Olivia says as we exit the station.

"Well, if it saves us some problems later on, it'll be worth it."

"I'd just like to know who was in my car last night." She unlocks the doors and looks around as if expecting to see another clue. But as usual, Olivia's car is tidy and clean.

"I guess we can rule out Garrett now." I get inside and buckle up. "Otherwise he wouldn't be willing to do the drug test."

"He wasn't exactly willing, Sam. I had to really talk him into it. Mostly he sounded seriously ticked. He's certain Jack planted that bag."

"Or it could've been a random act of stupidity," I point out. "I mean, since you left your car unlocked and there were lots of crazy kids at that party, anyone could've hopped in the back and done who knows what while we were inside the house."

"Ugh!" She glances into the backseat. "I'm going to ask my dad to get my car detailed ASAP!"

I'm tempted to tell Olivia about what Ebony just told me—the disappointing news that Zach might not be totally recovered yet—but I can't bring myself to say these words out loud. Instead, I tell myself that Zach will be different. He will beat this thing, once and for all. And just to be sure, I will be praying for him—regularly and fervently—to do so.

heard you got arrested last night," Conrad says to me when I answer my phone on Saturday afternoon.

"Hello to you too. And thanks for asking—I'm doing just fine. How about you?"

"Sorry. But I couldn't believe the news when Alex told me this morning, Sam. Did you and Olivia really get arrested when the party got busted?"

So, for like the umpteenth time, I tell my story, ending with, "but it looks like the charges will be dropped by Monday."

"That must've been exciting."

"Not as exciting as your basketball game, I'll bet." Okay, this is a low blow since I already know they lost by a pretty wide margin last night. But, hey, he was asking for it.

"Yeah, don't remind me. I'm just glad it was the last one. I was so ready to be done with it. What a cruddy season."

"So, we're both in a happy mood today?"

"I'm trying to put it behind me," he says. "I just called to see if you wanted a ride to youth group tonight. I thought we could grab something to eat first and sort of catch up, you know?"

"Sounds good." We talk a little more, then hang up, and I go downstairs and find Mom doing something on her laptop in the kitchen. I haven't told her what Ebony said about Zach yet. I'm not even sure I will.

"Are you working?" I ask, not wanting to interrupt her.

"No…" She looks up. "Just ordering a book online." She punches a key. "There, that should do it."

I take a soda out of the fridge and pop it open, trying to decide whether I should bring the subject up or not. "What book?" I ask, stalling.

"A new novel by Michael Crichton."

"Huh? You don't even like fiction, Mom. And Michael Crichton's books are all scientific and stuff. Why on earth would you order that?"

Now she gets a hard-to-read expression, almost like she's embarrassed. "A friend told me about it."

"A friend?" Suddenly I'm suspicious. "Which friend?"

"Well, you may as well know that I met a guy recently…"

My eyes get big. "A *guy*?"

"Now, don't go nuts on me here, Samantha."

"What kind of guy, Mom? I mean, is it anything serious?"

She sort of smiles now, but her cheeks are flushing in a very nonmomlike sort of way. "No, it's not serious, but I do like him. And I'm going on a date with him tonight."

"Really?"

She nods, then actually giggles.

"Where did you meet him?"

Now she frowns. "I knew you'd ask me that, Samantha. And not that it's any of your business, but Paula and I met him at the Second Street Pub."

"You've been going to the Second Street Pub? Isn't

that like a twenty-something, meat-market kind of place where people get drunk and hook up and have one-night stands and all that?"

"It might be for some people, but it's also a fun place for us *old-timers* too." She makes a face at me. "Just because I've passed forty doesn't mean I'm dead, Samantha. I can still enjoy live music and kick up my heels occasionally."

"You actually *dance*?" Okay, I don't know why I find this so shocking, but for some reason I *cannot* imagine my mom dancing, especially not with some stranger dude. The world is tilting ever so slightly just now.

She laughs. "Yes, I actually dance." She starts to shake her shoulders and shuffle her feet now. "You want me to show you a few steps?"

I hold up my hands to stop her. "No thanks, Mom. That's okay."

"Anyway, his name is Steven Lowry, and he's picking me up around seven. If you're here, I'll introduce you to him."

So I explain that I'll be gone with Conrad by then—*to youth group.* I don't tell her that I'd just as soon not meet this guy and that I hope it's nothing serious and that she will soon figure out the Second Street Pub isn't the smartest place to go around picking up boyfriends. But I keep my mouth shut.

"Well, maybe some other time then." She turns back to her laptop.

"Yeah, maybe so…" I stand there for a few moments as I consider telling her what Ebony told me about Zach's recovery, but then I realize Mom actually looks happy.

Strangely happy. And I'm not used to seeing her look like this. Despite my reservations about this Steven dude, I cannot bring myself to pop her balloon right now. "Have fun tonight," I say sort of lamely.

"You too, sweetie." She looks up at me. "But don't get arrested, okay?"

"Same back at you, Mom."

She gives me her best exasperated look, then just laughs.

"I better go get ready," I say as I head for the stairs. When I get to my room, I pick up my cell phone and open it. I'm curious enough about Mom's new "boyfriend" to call Conrad and cancel tonight so I can meet this guy. But then I stop. What difference would it really make? I mean, even if the guy had missing teeth and skull tattoos, was wearing black leather and a studded dog collar, even if he drove a Harley without a helmet—what could I possibly say that would change Mom's mind? Chances are, I would only make things worse. Still, as I get dressed for my evening and even as Conrad drives us to youth group, I can't help but wonder what Mom's new guy is like. I try not to let my imagination run away with me, but I guess I really am a little bit worried.

"Everything okay?" Conrad asks as he opens my door and helps me out of his car. He is such a gentleman!

"Huh?" I study him for a moment, taking in his curly red hair, which is cut short for basketball season, and his clear blue eyes. I can't help but return his goofy smile as I try to figure out what he's referring to.

"You were so quiet in the car," he continues. "Is everything okay? Did I say something to offend you?"

I shake my head and take his hand. "No, not at all. I guess I'm just obsessing over my mom and her new boyfriend."

"Your mom has a new boyfriend? What's he like?"

"That's just the problem. I don't have a clue. I haven't even seen him yet. All I know is that she met him at *the Second Street Pub.*"

"And *that's* got you worried."

"Well, yeah. I mean, wouldn't you be worried if it were your mom?"

He laughs. "Considering that my mom is married to my dad, sure, I'd be a little concerned."

"You're so lucky to have two normal parents."

"Guess that all depends on how you define *normal,* Sam. They can be pretty weird, if you ask me."

"You know what I mean."

He nods. "I guess I am lucky. My parents have their little fights and stuff, but mostly they're happy together. I know that's kinda unusual these days. Alex's parents aren't doing too well."

"Yeah, I heard they might get separated." I pause as he opens the door to the restaurant for me. We're doing Mexican tonight, and the smell is already making me hungry.

"It kinda looks that way."

"Poor Alex."

"He's taking it harder than you'd think."

After we're seated at the table, Conrad informs me that Alex wants to ask Olivia out again.

"Really?" I place the napkin in my lap.

"But he's worried she'll turn him down, like last time."

I laugh. "Isn't that a switch."

"Do you think she will?"

I consider this, remembering how Olivia had chased after Alex and then pined away when he rejected her. "Well, I have been coaching her on how to play hard to get, but I think she still likes him a lot."

"Maybe you can give her a hint," suggests Conrad. "Let her know that Alex might ask her out...and that he's feeling a little down because of his parents."

"You mean make her feel sorry for him? Like he's a sympathy case? Pity dating?"

Conrad frowns. "Well, not exactly."

"Sorry. I'll pass it along to her. And if I know Olivia, she'll handle it differently this time."

"Cool."

Then we order and just eat and talk about regular stuff, like regular kids doing regular things. And I remind myself of what Pastor Ken told me last month—about how I need balance in my life, how I can't take everything so seriously, and how I need to have some fun.

When we're done eating, I excuse myself to the ladies' room where, after using the facilities, I slip out my cell phone and call Olivia, giving her a quick heads-up about Alex.

"So are you saying no more playing hard to get with the boy?"

"Well...you don't want to look too eager, Livvie, but if you do want to go out with him, you'd better say yes this time. He might not have the confidence to ask again."

She laughs. "Gotcha!"

"See ya at youth group."

As it turns out, the timing was good, because before the evening is over, Alex and Olivia seem to be friendlier than usual. And the next day when she picks me up for church, she tells me Alex said he was interested in taking her out.

"And what did you say?"

"For starters, I didn't jump up and down and yell, 'Yes! Yes! Yes!' I was very relaxed about the whole thing, and I simply told him that sounded okay to me."

"You said it sounded *okay*?" I repeat. "Like curb your enthusiasm, girl."

She smiles. "Hey, he was fine with that."

"Well, good for him."

"And he suggested we go out with you and Conrad again."

"Cool."

"That's what I thought." She frowns now. "I was think-ing about something else too."

"What?"

"I think maybe I should quit Stewed Oysters."

"Yeah, I was wondering about that after what hap-pened on Friday night, especially if Jack was really involved."

"I'm going to tell Cameron tomorrow."

"Are you going to tell him why?"

"I think that's only fair."

"Well, good for you." I nod as she pulls into the church parking lot. "He needs to hear it. I mean, it's possible that Cameron isn't into any of that stuff, but if he keeps Jack in the band, it'll probably get them all into trouble."

"That's how I feel too." She turns off the car. "And my parents are adamant about it."

"You can't really blame them."

"So how did your mom's big date go last night?" she asks as we walk toward the church building. I told Olivia about it last night at youth group. I wanted her to pray for them.

"I'm not really sure. Mom got home after I went to bed. It was a little past midnight. But she didn't stumble in drunk and break something. And she was still asleep when I left this morning."

"Aren't you dying to meet this guy?"

"Actually, I'd rather not meet him."

"Huh?"

"I'm hoping it was just a one-time thing. I'd rather see my mom dating someone she didn't meet at a bar, you know what I mean?"

Olivia nods as we go inside. "Yeah, I totally get that."

"Sometimes it feels like I'm the parent and Mom is the kid," I whisper to her as we find seats.

Olivia squeezes my arm. "And you're such a good little mommy, Sam."

I laugh as we sit down. "Yeah, right."

Olivia drives me home from church, and we both notice a strange car in my driveway. "Who's at your house?" She pulls in behind it.

"I don't know." I study the small black sports car. "But that looks like a nice set of wheels."

"It's a BMW. And pretty new too, which means it was expensive. Hey, maybe it's your mom's new boyfriend— maybe he's loaded."

"Yeah, that thought occurred to me too..." I thank her for the ride, ask her to pray for me, and approach my house with more than a little hesitation. I am so not ready

for this. The thought of a strange man in my house…
dating my mom…sitting on our furniture…well, it's just
totally unnerving. I shoot up a silent prayer. *Dear God,
help me to be civilized and nice and friendly and kind and
not grumpy or rude or judgmental. Amen.*

Today's sermon was on hospitality and showing kind-
ness to strangers. It figures.

To my surprise, Steven Lowry appears to be all right. No tattoos (that I can see), no studded dog collars, or missing teeth. He has short, thick brown hair and dark, somewhat expressive eyes. He's clean-shaven and speaks intelligently. He's wearing pressed khakis, a white polo shirt, and moccasin loafers without socks, which means he's style conscious. Oh yeah, and his ankles are tan, and so are his arms and face, which means he's been somewhere warm and sunny lately since it's only March and, in the Northwest, not quite tanning weather yet. Or else he likes tanning booths, and call me conservative, but that just seems a little weird for a guy.

So anyway, he does seem sort of nice, and I'm thinking Mom has pretty good taste. Except for one thing—I'm not sure how old he is, but I suspect by the way he talks and acts that he's younger than she is. I'm guessing midthirties at the most. And he seems a little surprised when he meets me. Oh, he doesn't say as much, but I can see it in his eyes. Apparently she told him she has kids but didn't mention our ages. Anyway, I think he was expecting little kids. I wonder if she has told him about Zach…or rehab. I doubt it.

"So, how old are you, Samantha?" he asks as we all sit in the family room drinking iced tea that my mom must've made before I got here.

"Seventeen. I'm a junior."

He nods, then turns to my mom. "How old is your son, Beth? I forgot his name already."

"Zachary. He's twenty." She doesn't mention anything about rehab, and I can tell by the look she tosses my way that I better not either.

Steven's brows lift ever so slightly, then he smiles. "You must've been a child yourself when you had children."

She laughs as she pushes back a strand of her recently highlighted hair, something I encouraged as a way to cover the gray that had made her look even older than forty-one. "Actually, I was a little young by today's standards. But back then I thought I was fairly grown-up."

Does she think by saying this it'll magically shave off a few years? I mean, I know girls my age who've had babies, but add twenty years to that, and you still get thirty-seven. But thirty-seven probably sounds a lot better to my mom than forty-one. Especially if Steven is like thirty-one, which seems entirely possible.

"So, what do you do, Steven?" I ask, suddenly feeling like I've become the "man" of the house and am asking my daughter's new beau whether his intentions are honorable or not.

"I'm a financial planner."

"Is that sort of like a stockbroker?"

He smiles. "That and a few other things too—insurance, mutual funds. I try to help people build a solid financial plan that ensures a comfortable future."

"And have you lived in Brighton long?" I decide to continue my little inquisition. What can it hurt?

"No, actually, I'm a newcomer."

"Really?" I glance at Mom to see whether she's taking offense at my line of questioning, but she actually looks slightly amused, which I interpret as a green light. "Where did you move from?"

"Southern California." He shakes his head. "It was getting too crazy down there for me. Too many people on the beaches, too much traffic on the highways. So I decided to check out the beautiful Northwest, and after a couple of weeks here last fall, I decided I liked it. Lucky for me, my company had an office up here, and I was transferred last month."

I guess that explains the tan. "So, you must not have any family or ties to keep you in California then?" Okay, this is my way of trying to determine if the guy's been married or has any children.

"I have some family down there. My mom's still in Pasadena, and I have a brother and his wife in San Diego. But that's about it." He glances at Mom now. "Your daughter would make a good detective."

Mom just smiles. "She takes after her dad."

He slowly nods with an expression that tells me he's already heard about my dad being a cop and about how he died.

"And since I'm new in town," he continues, "I was really happy to get to know your mom and her friend Paula. Other than my co-workers, who all seem to have lives of their own, I don't really know anyone here yet."

"I hope you like it here," I say as I stand up. Somehow I think it's time for me to give this guy a break.

"Yes, I warned him that we get a lot of rain," says Mom.

"It's too gloomy for some people," I say as I head to the kitchen to drop off my glass.

"I'm looking forward to it," he says as I come back through.

Then I tell him it was nice to meet him and excuse myself to go upstairs. As I leave, I think I see a wave of relief washing over my mom's face. Well, what did she expect me to do? Welcome him with open arms? Give him the keys to the castle? At least I didn't tell the poor guy about Zachary's drug problems or how I get visions from God or how old Mom really is. Honestly, it could've gone much, much worse.

On Monday morning Amanda's sweet-sixteen party is the hot topic at school. I'm not sure if Amanda is as pleased as she thought she'd be, since I heard her parents grounded her for an undetermined amount of time. But to be fair, I think they should ground themselves as well. I mean, what kind of parents throw a huge party like that for high-school kids and then take off? What were they thinking? As it turns out, some kids really did get into trouble. A lot of the alcohol and substance charges will probably stick. It sounds like a fair number of kids will probably be taking mandatory diversion classes—where the system teaches them about the effects of alcohol abuse. Unfortunately, I suspect that some of the hard-core users got away without being arrested. But that's probably the way it usually goes.

"How'd the test go on Saturday?" I ask Garrett in

chem class. Of course, I'm talking about the drug test, but for his sake I'm trying to be discreet.

He gives me a totally blank look.

"You know…" I lower my voice. "At the police station."

He rolls his eyes. "I didn't go in."

"Why not?"

He shrugs. "Why should I have to prove my innocence? Let them prove that I'm guilty first."

"But it could've gotten you off, Garrett. Olivia and I both did the test."

He looks surprised. "Why?"

"Because we wanted the charges dropped."

Then the bell rings, and Mr. Dynell begins to lecture. As I listen to Dynell, I can't help but fume at Garrett. Why didn't he go in and take that stupid test? It would've been so easy. I glare at him, but he's not looking at me. And suddenly I start to wonder if he might've had a reason not to go in. Maybe he really does have a drug problem and knew he'd flunk that test.

I try to block worries about Garrett from my mind as I attempt to understand what Dynell is saying about dimensional analysis—like I even get it.

But really, what's the point in obsessing over Garrett and his problems? It's not like I can do anything about it anyway. And thinking about him not taking that test only frustrates me. Who needs the stress? So I decide to just put all this crud behind me. Oh, sure, I'll pray for Garrett. And I'll be his friend and lab partner. But when it comes to his personal life, he's on his own. Well, unless he asks for my help, that is. Otherwise, I'm going to focus on my own life for a change.

By Wednesday, the charges for both Olivia and me

have been dropped. Of course, that's not the case with Garrett. Still, he doesn't seem terribly concerned. So I continue to put it out of my mind as well. Besides, Zach comes home tomorrow, and I want to put my energy into making his homecoming special.

Mom and I talked to him on the phone Tuesday night, and he sounded so happy, so positive about his future and seeing his family again. I can't wait to see him. Mom started crying when she was talking to him. I guess he said some really touching things, and then he had both of us on the line and sincerely apologized to us, asking us to forgive him and promising to make things right for himself and for us. We both reassured him that we've forgiven him and just want to move on. We all want to return to a "normal" life again.

After school on Thursday, Olivia comes over to help decorate our house for our little homecoming party. It looks a little juvenile with the balloons and streamers and things, but at least it's cheerful. Then Olivia sticks around to finish things up while Mom and I drive out to the airport to get Zach. I wanted to invite a bunch of people over for this, but because of Zach's crazy lifestyle before he went to rehab, it's hard to know who his "good" friends really are. Finally I decided to keep it small. I invited Olivia, since she's sort of like family and Zach's known her for years and actually likes her. I also invited his best friend from high school. I'm sure Zach will be surprised by this. But it seemed like fate, or God, when I happened to run into Tate Mitchell at the grocery store on Monday.

I assumed Tate would still be away at college, but it turns out he decided to take some time off after Christmas.

"I just need to figure out my life before I finish my schooling," he explained to me in the produce section. Then I told him a little about Zach and the whole rehab thing. I figured Zach wouldn't mind because he and Tate used to be pretty close, and Tate was always one of those trust-worthy sort of friends. Tate seemed really concerned about Zach and wanted to reconnect with him, so I invited him to our little welcome-home party.

"It'd be great to see Zach," said Tate. "It has been kinda lonely around town."

So I'm feeling pretty good as Mom and I drive to the Portland airport together. Life is about to get a lot better for our little family. Of course, I also remember Ebony's warning, although I don't think that's going to be the case with Zach. I still haven't mentioned to Mom what Ebony said. For one thing there hasn't been an appropriate moment, but perhaps more than that, it's something I just really don't want to think about. Perhaps it's better for everyone to take a positive approach anyway. One thing I know for sure—I'm not about to tell Mom right now. She looks truly happy, and there's no point in raining on her parade over something that probably won't even happen.

We wait in the baggage-claim area as planned, and I can hardly believe it when we see Zach walking toward us with his backpack slung over one shoulder. He looks dif-ferent. Older and more grown-up and surprisingly like Dad. And he's smiling so big you'd think he'd just won the lottery. His clothing looks neat and clean, and it appears he's put on some weight, which is good. His face has filled out some, and his eyes look clear and bright and happy. We all rush toward each other, falling into a group hug.

Then as we step back from each other, we're all wiping tears from our faces. Seriously, I think this is one of the best moments we've had in years. I pause for a couple of seconds, just staring at my brother as though I'm seeing someone who's come back from the dead.

"Zach," I finally admit, "when I first saw you, I almost thought you were Dad. You look so much like him. I guess I never noticed it before."

Mom is blowing her nose and nodding. "I thought the same thing."

Zach smiles even bigger now. "Thanks."

I keep looking at him as we head over to the baggage carousel to collect his bag. "You look fantastic!"

Mom hooks her arm into his. "You really do, Zach. It's so great to have you back. I mean, *really* back."

"It's good to be back. You have no idea how good."

He gets his duffel bag, and we head for the car, then home. We're all talking and catching up, and it really feels awesome to be a family like this again. It feels like it's long overdue, and I so look forward to getting to know my brother all over again. He's amazingly open about his addiction problems and how much the treatment program has helped him. He sounds so assured and confident that I have no doubt Ebony's brother must run a first-rate facility. And as we go over a bridge a few miles from town, I am compelled to silently thank God for this amazing intervention.

I sit contentedly in the backseat as Zach tells us about some of the hiking expeditions and outdoor challenges they had in Washington during rehab. I can't wait to tell Ebony how well it has gone for him—and to thank her. I almost invited her to join us for the welcome-home party, but I wasn't sure how Zach would react to having her there since she pressured him into going in the first place. The last time he saw Ebony, he looked like he wanted to kill her. But that's all changed now. It's plain to see that Zach is a totally new person.

He's a little surprised to find Olivia and Tate waiting at home for us, but he seems pleased too. "You guys did all this for me?" He looks at the banner and balloons and food. "You're making me feel like that old prodigal son in the Bible. Remember how he came home expecting to live in the barn and work for wages but they threw him a big feast instead?"

"We're just so glad that you're home and well." Mom hugs him again. "That's worth celebrating."

Tate and Zach seem to pick up right where they left off. Tate asks Zach about his recovery program, and Zach spares no details. "It was really rough at first. Going through detox is like going through hell. Seriously, man, you just want to die."

Tate frowns. "Sounds pretty bad."

"Yeah, at one point I was ready to make a run for it."

"What stopped you?"

Zach shrugs. "For one thing, it was winter, and the weather was pretty bad right then. But I really thought about stuff, and I sort of figured rehab was my only chance at a real life again. If I'd bolted, there probably would've been a warrant for me, and if they'd caught me, I'd be stuck in jail."

Tate asks why, and Zach explains about how his car had been found with some compromising evidence. Tate just nods like he understands. Then Mom pipes up and tells Zach about how Olivia and I recently found ourselves in a similar position. Naturally, Zach is stunned.

"No way!" He looks at me and then her. "You two couldn't possibly get into that kind of crud! Oh, tell me it ain't so."

So we relate the whole story of the birthday party and the Ziploc baggie in Olivia's backseat and how embarrassing it was to be arrested—clear up to how the charges were finally dropped for both of us just yesterday.

"That's too bad you had to go through all that," he says. "But at least you were innocent."

"Even so," I say, "it was pretty scary being taken into custody like that and then questioned like we were serious criminals."

"Tell me about it." Zach nods. "Makes a person want to stay outta trouble for good."

"Yes," agrees my mom. "That would make me happy too."

We visit awhile longer, and then Tate and Zach decide to drive around town. "Just to see what it feels like being on the outside again," Zach tells us. "If you guys don't mind."

Mom waves him off. "Go," she says happily. "Enjoy your freedom. You've worked hard for it."

I nod. "Yeah, we're just glad you're home and back on track. Have some fun."

"I should go too," says Olivia. "I have to cram for tomorrow's lit exam."

And then, once again, it's just Mom and me rattling around the house. But this time it feels different. It's not so depressing. And I can hear Mom humming as she puts dishes in the dishwasher. It's like we've entered into a new chapter of our lives together as a family, and I can't help but think things are going to be better. A lot better.

Six

So how's Zach doing?" Olivia asks as she drives us to school. It's Friday, and my brother's been home for just over a week now. It started out so good, but lately I've been a little unsure. Oh, I don't like to worry, but I just don't know.

"Okay," I tell her. But even as I say this, I'm not convinced.

"Okay, as in good? Or just okay?"

Olivia knows me, and I figure I should just be honest with her. "I guess I'm a little worried about him."

"Has he gone to an NA meeting yet?"

I shake my head and mutter, "No." I already explained to her how Zach is supposed to attend Narcotics Anonymous meetings three times a week. It's part of his recovery program. Also, he's supposed to meet with his mentor, a guy named Casey, who has called our house at least once a day during the past week, but as far as I know, they haven't gotten together once.

"Why not?"

"Well, at first Zach told us he just needed a break from all that. He said after three months and so many meetings and group counseling sessions and therapy and stuff, he was just tired of it."

"That's understandable."

"Maybe, but what if he doesn't go at all?"

"So he's had his week off. Maybe your mom can put some pressure on him to get back into the routine now."

"Yeah...maybe...but she's kind of distracted with Steven too."

"They're still dating?"

"Yeah. That's another part of the problem."

"What?"

"Zach doesn't really like Steven."

"Oh."

"I mean, I have to give Zach some credit. He hasn't let my mom know how he feels. But he has told me that he thinks Steven is a fake."

"A fake?"

"Yeah. That's what I said too."

"What does Zach mean?"

"He thinks Steven is pretending to be something he's not. He thinks he's some kind of con man and that he's going to take advantage of Mom somehow."

"Seriously?"

"Pretty weird, huh?"

"So what do you think about Steven?"

"Well, I told you how I was sort of suspicious of him at first. He's younger than Mom, and I wondered why a guy who has never been married, drives a cool car, makes good money...well, you know, why would he be interested in an older woman, especially one with two kids? Okay, nearly grown kids. But still I wondered...at least at first anyway."

"But your mom's a pretty cool lady," says Olivia. "She's

smart and good looking, especially after that makeover. Why wouldn't he like her?"

"I know. And after getting to know Steven a little better, I've begun to like him. And I can see that he really is good for my mom. He treats her well, and she seems happier having him in her life."

"You'd think Zach would appreciate that."

"You'd think, but I'm starting to wonder if Zach is jealous."

"Seriously?"

"Yeah, I think he might've gotten the idea that he would come home and be the man of the house and take care of things. And then he finds out Mom's already got a man. Or sort of. I mean, it's not like they're serious or anything. But you know. It's like Zach's role has been taken."

"So does Zach know what he wants to do now that he's back?"

"Mom keeps encouraging him to register for classes at the community college. She thought he could still get in for spring term. But he keeps making excuses. He says he'd rather work for a while."

"Nothing wrong with that," Olivia says as we get out of the car.

"No, but it's not like he's been looking for a job either."

"Well, it's only been a week. Maybe he just needed some time to chill, you know, after getting out of the cooler." She laughs at her joke, then looks sorry. "Not that he was in prison exactly. But after the way he described the place, I'm guessing it might've felt like that sometimes."

I nod as I sling the strap of my bag over my shoulder. "You're probably right." And part of me really does believe that's it. Zach just needed a break. Now that he's had a week off, he'll probably get back on track, and everything will be fine.

Garrett and I have been in something of a standoff this week. I mean, we're still lab partners and everything, but our conversation has been a little stilted. At first I thought it was me chilling him out since I was irked that he refused to take that drug test. But then it seemed like he was the one giving me the cold shoulder.

"So are you going to be mad at me forever?" he finally asks as we sit across the table staring blankly at each other before chem class starts.

"I'm not mad."

He rolls his eyes.

"Okay, I just don't know why you wouldn't want to get the charges dropped."

He shrugs. "It's my life, and I happen to believe in my rights and that I am supposed to be innocent until someone *proves* me guilty."

"But why go through all that when you could've gotten off like Olivia and me?"

"I'll get off," he assures me.

"Whatever."

"Did Olivia quit the band like she said she was going to?"

I nod as I take a pen out of my bag. "She told Cameron why she was quitting, and he was really bummed."

"If he's that bummed, maybe he should lose Jack McAllister."

"Olivia said that Cameron said Jack doesn't do meth."

"Yeah, right."

"Seriously," I tell him. "Cameron seemed pretty sure of it."

"Then Cameron is in deep denial."

I study Garrett as Mr. Dynell goes to the front of the class. "How can you be so sure?" I ask, but the bell rings, and it's time for another exciting chem test. TGIF. Still, I wonder what makes Garrett such an expert. I also continue to wonder if there's another reason he refused to take the drug test. Maybe sometime, when we have more time, I'll ask him specifically.

After school, Olivia drops me off at the police station. Ebony asked me to come in and discuss some things with her. As it turns out, the department is creating a task force to really focus on the growing meth problem in our community.

"Because of that dream you had," Ebony tells me, "which I assume was meth related, I think you should be on the task force."

"Sure. I'd like to be."

"Naturally, this is an internal task force. No one on the outside should be aware of your involvement. The chief will be especially pleased to learn that someone from the high school will be participating."

I consider this. "Does that make me a narc?"

She frowns. "That just comes with the department territory, Samantha. I assumed you knew that."

I nod. "I guess I do know that. But sometimes I need a reminder." I force a smile. "It's like I have a double life, you know? High-school student by day, secret agent by night."

Ebony laughs. "Well, the main goal of the task force isn't to nail high-school kids who are using," she explains. "Not that addiction issues don't concern us. They do.

But what we want to do is to backtrack up the drug line until we find the ones at the top. The manufacturers and distributors. That's where we want to make some big arrests."

"I always thought that meth came from somewhere else," I say. "I mean, we always hear about the I-5 Corridor, and I figured it was coming up here from California or Mexico or someplace far away."

"A lot of people figure that same thing, and it's partially true, but we have reason to believe that a fair amount of the substance is coming from right here in Brighton."

"Oh…"

"That's why we're taking this all very seriously."

I nod.

"They did some more testing on the meth residue in the baggie from Olivia's car. We have reason to believe it was locally manufactured as well."

"Really?"

"And we would love to find out who put that in Olivia's car." She leans forward now. "Do you have any ideas?"

"To be honest, I'd kind of put it out of my mind."

"I can understand that. But I'd like you to give it some thought." She leans back and sighs now. "I guess I'm even hoping that God might help you out on this. It's disturbing to think that high-school kids are getting drugs from local manufacturers."

"Why?"

"Oh, I suppose it's because it makes getting meth seem so much easier, so much more accessible." She shakes her head.

"Well, I'll do what I can."

Ebony gives me a notebook with some printed material

in it. "Go over this information when you can. There'll be a task-force meeting on Wednesday."

I thank her, and she asks how Zach is doing. I smile and act like everything is okay, and she nods and seems pleased. But as I leave the police station, I feel like a liar and a hypocrite. This is Ebony, my trusted friend and Dad's old partner. She deserves my honesty. So why didn't I tell her the truth? Maybe it's like Olivia said. Maybe it's too soon to jump to conclusions. It's only been a week, and Zach probably just needed a break. I'm sure he'll get it together by the beginning of next week. Perhaps he's meeting with Casey right now. Or maybe he'll attend an NA meeting this weekend. I happen to know, since I studied the schedule, that there's one at a local church on Saturday night. Maybe I can encourage him to go. I could even offer to go with him. I've heard that it's good for family members to get involved.

But on Saturday morning when I attempt to encourage him in this direction, he sort of shuts me down. Not in a rude way exactly. But he informs me that he and Tate already have plans for Saturday evening.

"Have you met with your sponsor yet?"

He frowns at me. "No offense, Sam, but you're starting to sound like a nag."

"I'm sorry. It's just that I care about you, Zach."

He smiles. "I know you do. And I promise that first thing next week I will start going to NA, and I'll meet with Casey."

"Really?"

He nods. "You happy now?"

"Yes, thanks." And so I feel hopeful.

"Hey, Zach, how's the job search going?" Mom asks

him a little later when we all happen to be in the kitchen at the same time.

"Okay," he says as he stares into the refrigerator with his back toward her.

"Meaning?" Mom stands behind him, waiting, I'm sure, for a more complete answer. She hasn't said anything specifically yet, but I think she's getting impatient with Zach. And I suspect she's a little worried too.

"Meaning...I have some good prospects."

"Where?"

He turns and looks at her, and it's hard to read his expression. "Here and there." Then he takes out a soda, closes the refrigerator door, and walks out of the kitchen.

Mom frowns. "I hope he's taking this seriously," she says to me as she pours a cup of coffee.

I nod. "I think he is." But even as I say this, I'm not totally sure. I guess I just want to believe that it's true. If Zach wasn't in the family room right now, I'd use this opportunity to tell Mom what Ebony said to me a few weeks ago. As it is, I don't really want him to hear me saying something so negative.

Besides, it's not like he's done anything wrong. I think we're all a little apprehensive. And I know it's hard to figure out what our roles are with each other after having been apart. I mean, I want to encourage Zach to go to meetings and to talk to his mentor, but how do I do that without sounding like a nag? Mostly I think I need to pray for Zach. I need to ask God to continue the healing miracle that has already begun in his life. I pray that Zach will succeed and make everyone proud. I know, with God, this is within the realm of possibility.

s that Tate and Zach?" Olivia asks after we exit the movie theater on Sunday night. Conrad and I are double-dating with Olivia and Alex. It's their first "official" date as a couple, and I can tell that Olivia is being careful not to act overly interested.

I glance over to where a couple of guys are getting into a dark-colored Toyota across the street, but it's rainy and dark, and I can't see them well enough to be sure. "That does look like Tate's car," I say as we huddle underneath the awning, waiting for Conrad and Alex to bring the Gremlin by to pick us up.

"I wonder what they're doing over there?" Olivia peers at the run-down apartment complex on the other side of the street.

"Maybe Tate lives there," I suggest, although I had assumed he was living at home to save money. The Toyota pulls away just as Conrad's bright orange Gremlin pulls up.

"Our chariot awaits," says Olivia, and we dash over and hop in.

As the three of them discuss the movie, which I thought was a little lame, my mind is elsewhere. Primarily on Zach and Tate. What are they up to tonight? And does Tate really live in one of those grungy apartments? Somehow it just doesn't fit with his image. Although I could be all wrong about that guy. The more I think about it, the more I really do wonder about him.

Even though Tate works at his uncle's automotive store, he and Zach have really been hanging together a lot this past week. Tate's often at our house when I come home from school. I wonder how he has time to work. Maybe that's part of the reason Zach hasn't gotten a job yet.

I feel partially responsible for bringing Tate into the picture with Zach, but I'd assumed he was a "safe" friend. Now I'm not so sure. For one thing, I suspect he and Zach have been drinking together. Naturally, this is a huge concern, because drug addicts are supposed to avoid alcohol. Just from what I've recently read for the task force, I know that alcohol is a gateway to more addictive drugs. Especially for teens. And earlier this week I thought I smelled alcohol on Zach's breath. But he was also chewing mint gum, so I couldn't be sure, and then I convinced myself I was just being paranoid.

But last night after I got home from youth group and while Mom was still out with Steven, Tate dropped Zach at home. It wasn't that late, not quite eleven, but when Zach walked through the kitchen, I felt fairly certain he'd been drinking. I could smell it, and he was acting a little funny. I asked him about it, and he got pretty defensive.

"Look," he said with an offended expression, "I know you're a Christian and have really high moral standards, Sam. And that's great for you. But you can't expect me to live up to them too. I mean, I know I blew it with drugs, and I'm not going back there. But I can't live like a saint either."

"No one expects you to be a saint. I just don't want you to blow it now." I softened my tone. "I really care about you, Zach."

He sort of smiled then. "Thanks, Sis. I appreciate that. Just don't worry so much, okay?"

And that was pretty much the end of it. I decided I should tell Mom, but so far I haven't had the chance. She wasn't up when I went to church this morning, and then she and Steven had taken off to the coast by the time I got home afterward. They were still gone when I left for the movie tonight.

"You're being pretty quiet, Sam," Olivia says from the backseat.

"Yeah," Conrad says as he pulls into his favorite burger joint. We all agreed to have a late dinner tonight. "The movie was that bad, huh?"

I sort of laugh. "Well, it wasn't fantastic." But then, not wanting to sound like a complainer, I tell them about the part I actually did like. And I push my worries about Zach and Tate from my mind as we go inside and sit down. We laugh and joke, and I'm so thankful that I have such good friends. I just wish my brother did too. I've asked him to go to church or youth group, but he refuses.

"Cameron Vincent called me this afternoon," Olivia says after our food arrives.

"Why?" Alex asks in a slightly jealous tone.

"He wants me back in the band."

"I thought you told him why you couldn't stay with them," I say as I squirt ketchup on my fries.

Olivia's eyes get big. "He told me he kicked Jack out. He said he agreed with me about him."

"No way," says Conrad.

"I thought he was positive that Jack wasn't doing drugs," I point out.

"I thought so too," says Olivia. "Guess he changed his mind."

"But you're not going back with them, are you?" asks Alex.

"I don't know…" Olivia looks perplexed. "I mean, I told Cameron I'd think about it…and pray about it…but I'm not really sure."

"It seems like an invitation for trouble," says Alex.

"Or an opportunity to share your faith," I suggest.

She nods. "Yeah. That's what I was thinking."

"And you have to hand it to Cameron for kicking Jack out," I add.

"But man, is Jack going to be mad at you now," says Alex. "You might be needing a bodyguard, Olivia." He winks at her. "Maybe I should apply for that position."

"I'll get back to you on that," she teases.

As they continue to joke about all this, I begin to put together a plan. I'm thinking that since I'm on the drug task force, I might be able to do a little surveil-lance work around school. I know Ebony said that the police aren't focusing their attention on teens who use drugs but rather on those who make and sell the crud. Still, if I could track Jack's whereabouts, maybe it would lead somewhere. The only problem is that I don't have a car. And Ebony said my involvement in the task force is supposed to be covert, so I'm not sure I can tell Olivia about it. I'll call Ebony tomorrow for some more clarification.

Because it's Sunday and tomorrow's a school day, we call it a night. When I get home, I'm not surprised to see that Zach is still out. But I'm thankful Mom is back now.

"How was the coast?" I give my damp jacket a shake and then hang it on a hook by the door.

She frowns. "Even wetter than here."

"Too bad."

"But we had a nice lunch."

"How's Steven doing?" I sit down across the breakfast bar from Mom, watching as she dips a tea bag up and down in her mug.

She squeezes her tea bag, then sets it on a napkin. "He's okay." She nods toward the tea kettle on the stove. "That water's still hot if you want some tea or cocoa or something."

So I get out a tea bag and pour a mug full of water and come back to join her, hoping this might be my chance to raise my concerns about Zach.

"How was the movie?"

I shrug. "Not so great. We think we saw Zach and Tate afterward."

She brightens a little. "Were they at the movie too?"

So I explain how they were over by the apartment complex. "But they might've parked there for the movie," I tell her, although I know it's a no-parking zone.

"Steven is convinced that Zach doesn't like him."

"Really?" I study her expression and wonder if this is why she looks kind of bummed. "Why's that?"

"Well, remember when they met on Wednesday?

Steven said that Zach said some things that sounded like a hint."

"A hint?"

"You know, like 'leave my mom alone.'" She sort of laughs. "Although Steven is taking it pretty well. He said that he thinks it's a fairly normal response and that he'd probably act the same way under those circumstances."

"Is that why he hasn't been around here much lately?"

She nods, then takes a sip of tea.

"I'm a little worried about Zach, Mom…"

She doesn't say anything, just keeps looking down at her tea, but I can see her frown lines deepening.

I consider telling her my suspicions about his alcohol use, but that feels like tattling. So I tell her about Ebony's warning instead.

"Yes…" She looks up at me. "I've heard the same thing, Sam."

"So, are you worried?"

She sighs. "Well, naturally, but I'm trying to stay positive."

"I did talk to him," I say. "I asked him why he wasn't going to NA meetings or talking to his sponsor."

"And?"

"He said he's going to start next week. He told me not to worry."

"Then maybe you shouldn't."

"Yeah, that's what I keep telling myself. That I should pray instead of worry. And for the most part, I do. It's just that I feel a little guilty."

"*You* feel guilty?"

"Because I kind of helped to reconnect him with Tate. And now I'm not so sure about Tate."

"Tate's a nice kid, Sam. I'm glad they're doing things together. I think Tate's good for Zach."

"Really?"

"Yes, Tate seems to have his head on straight. I even like the fact that he's taken time off from school just to be sure that he's picked the right major. He didn't want to waste his parents' money. That shows real maturity. And there's nothing wrong with getting experience in the business world."

"I guess so." Maybe I'm all wrong about Tate. Maybe I am just getting paranoid.

Mom smiles now. "And you need to remember that you're the youngest one in this family, Samantha. It's not up to you to take care of the rest of us. Just relax and have fun…enjoy being a kid, okay?"

"I do."

"Speaking of fun, Steven invited us to go skiing with him next Saturday. All this rain down here is translating into some good spring skiing up at Hood. You interested?"

"Sure. Sounds fun."

"Great. Plan on it. Hopefully Zach will want to come too. I think it'd be a good way for him and Steven to get better acquainted."

"I'd be surprised if he didn't want to come," I tell her. "I don't think he has been snowboarding since high school."

"Then maybe you could encourage him to join us." She stands and puts her mug in the sink, looks at the clock, and tells me good night.

I consider this as she heads upstairs. On one hand,

Zach *should* be glad to go snowboarding. On the other hand, what will it be like for Zach and Steven to be stuck together for an entire day? What if they get into some kind of ugly squabble?

Eight

F or the sake of the task force, I think you should keep your involvement quiet," Ebony says as I meet with her on Monday afternoon.

"I sort of thought that was what you'd say, and I haven't told Olivia. I've also been thinking I'd like to do a little surveillance work."

Ebony sort of smiles. "What kind of surveillance work?"

So I explain my idea about tracking some of the kids at school, ones like Jack, who are probably involved in drugs. "Not to catch them, but just to see who they might be connected to—maybe even the dealers, you know?"

"That could be dangerous, Samantha."

"I know. But I think I could do it without drawing attention. Especially since I'm just a kid like them. We end up at the same kinds of places a lot of the time anyway. I doubt they'd even notice me. And I'd be careful."

"We'd have to put you through some sort of surveillance training."

"Great!"

"That is, if the powers that be would agree to such a crazy idea, which remains to be seen. Also, we'd have to get your mother's approval... Oh, I don't know, Sam."

"Look, Ebony," I plead with her. "I want to be a cop. I'm on the drug task force. And you said yourself that this is a problem that hurts kids my age. Plus I've already been in some pretty dangerous spots."

Her brow creases as she considers this. "Those are good points. And if you're going to continue working with us, you really will need more training." She goes to her bookshelf and retrieves a book called *Secrets of Surveillance.* "You might try studying this for starters, not that I can promise you anything, but I will talk to the chief and get back to you."

"Tell him I'd be really careful, and remind him that I've already been in some tight spots and that some additional training would be good—"

"Yes, yes, I think I got that already."

"But you're not taking it seriously?" I frown.

"I am taking it seriously, Sam. And I like the fact that you're taking it seriously too. And I would like to see our town get a handle on this problem before it becomes an even worse crisis."

"So maybe it's possible?"

"Maybe..." She picks up a pen and turns it around in her hand. "But you'd have to be able to keep your identity completely secret. Other than your mother, no one can know."

"Not even Olivia?"

She shakes her head. "And this is all assuming that we get approval, Sam."

"But if I can't tell Olivia...," I say, sort of thinking out loud. "I mean, she's my main mode of transportation. Other than my bike, that is." Okay, it's embarrassing to admit this. But it's the truth. I grin at Ebony. "I guess I'll just have to do my surveillance on foot."

Ebony chuckles, then nods. "That would make it difficult."

"I have been saving for a car, and getting paid from the police department will help too. But I can't really afford one yet."

"Well, before you get all worried about a vehicle, you'd better let me do a little research around here and see if this is even viable." She makes a note of something, and suddenly I'm worried that she might set me up in one of those "unmarked" police cars that are so obviously police cars. I almost say this, but that might sound insulting since she drives one. Besides, I really am jumping the gun here. It's possible this whole surveillance idea will be shot down by the end of the day.

We talk a little more. She asks about Zach, and I tell her that everything's fine. I do this for several reasons: one, I don't want to sound ungrateful for her intervention and her brother's rehab facility; two, I don't want to admit that Zach isn't doing that well; and, three, I'm hoping things will change, and I'm trying to give my brother the benefit of the doubt.

"That's great, Samantha. I was really praying for him last week. I'm glad to hear it's going well."

So we say good-bye, and I go back outside to where Olivia's waiting for me. She's talking on her phone but finishes up as I get in the car.

"That was Cameron," she says as I fasten my seat belt.

"What's up?"

"I told him I'd come back to the band." She starts the car. "But with the understanding that I am totally out of there if drugs or alcohol are being used."

"And he's okay with that?"

"He said he was."

"I didn't see Jack at school today. How about you?"

"Trust me, I was keeping a lookout for that dude. And I didn't see him at all until the end of the day. I noticed him standing out by the west exit, smoking a cigarette."

"Maybe he's just keeping a low profile."

"He was with that new girl, the one with the motorcycle jacket, the electric blue bangs, and attitude."

"She's in my journalism class," I tell her. "She transferred here from Madison last month. Her name is Felicity, and she acts like she has an attitude, but I think she's just shy."

"Sorry," says Olivia. "I didn't mean to sound like a snob."

"I've been trying to be nice to her. She seems a little depressed, and it can't be easy switching schools. But I'm disappointed to hear she's hanging with Jack."

"Well, they looked happy together." Olivia sort of laughs.

I don't respond to this. It's just as wrong for me to judge Jack as it is for Olivia to judge Felicity. Sometimes I feel like a pathetic example of a Christian.

"Maybe Felicity will be a good distraction for Jack. I'm sure he's seriously ticked about being dropped from the band. I just hope he's not mad at me personally."

"You might want to take Alex up on his bodyguard offer."

She laughs. "Yeah, I was thinking the same thing. But maybe Jack and Felicity will fall madly in love, and he'll forget all about his botched music career."

"I still wonder if it was Jack who put that Ziploc bag in your car," I say as she stops for a light.

"He seems the most obvious suspect."

"Unless it was Garrett…" Okay, I feel sort of bad to say this out loud, but it's too late.

"*Not* Garrett," she says quickly. "I cannot imagine that sweet boy using something as hideous as meth. It's just so wrong."

I try not to take offense on behalf of Zach now. But I do get quieter.

"So is Ebony putting you on a new case?" she asks after driving a few blocks.

"Not exactly. Mostly we were just catching up."

"Oh…"

I don't go into any sort of explanation. And I do feel kind of bad for shutting her out, but I can't figure any other way to handle it. I'm so used to telling Olivia everything, and suddenly it feels like I can't tell her anything. I mean, I can't talk about the task force or my desire to do surveillance work. And I don't really want to talk about my concerns for Zach, since that might make it seem like he's a failure, confirming her prejudices regarding meth addicts.

So I just keep my mouth closed until we get to my house. Then I thank her for the ride and go inside to find Zach and Tate sitting in the family room watching a DVD that looks pretty violent and raunchy to me. They don't say anything to me, and I ignore them, going straight up to my room, where I flop onto my bed, close my eyes, and try to imagine what a "normal" family might be like.

And then I start to get that sensation, that buzzing feeling. It's like the room is turning, and that's when I see something blue. As though a camera lens is focusing, the splotch of blue slowly grows clearer, and I see that it's actually Felicity's bangs hanging down over her forehead and obscuring her eyes. She's lying on an old red sofa with one hand limply draped over her mouth, and the other arm seems to be twisted behind her back in a way that looks pretty uncomfortable. Her face is very pale, and she's not moving. And then I see what looks like a hypodermic syringe off to one side, along with a spoon and a candle stub. I'm not exactly sure of the meaning of all these items, but I suspect they're drug related. Then just like that, the vision disappears, and I sit up and look around my room to see that all is normal.

I go online to do some research. I guess I just need to confirm that what I saw really was drug related. I assume it's meth. But then, after reading some pretty disgusting details, I know for certain. Now what am I supposed to do? Should I warn Felicity? And if I do warn her, how will she react? Will she think I'm a narc? Will she stop talking to me? The only way to figure this out will be to pray for help. If God gave me that vision about Felicity, He must plan on giving me the means to help her. So I get down on my knees, and I really pray for her.

"Dear heavenly Father, I believe You've shown me that Felicity is in serious danger, and I really do want to help her. I just don't know what to do…where to begin. But You know what to do, and You care about her—so much so that You gave me this vision. Please protect Felicity. Keep her safe until she can get some serious help. And help me to continue befriending her. Help me to win her trust. Show me what to do and how to do it. Please lead me and guide me. I really do want to serve You. I really do want to love Felicity the way You love her. But I need Your help. Amen."

By Wednesday, I think maybe Felicity is beginning to trust me. Without going into all the details, I clue Olivia in to the fact that God has shown me this girl needs help. We even ask her to eat lunch with us, but she declines our invite so she can hang with Jack. I try not to sound negative about Jack, because he's the first one who really reached out to her, and she likes him.

Later in the day, Garrett seems extra quiet. And in chemistry, he almost completely ignores me. I try to convince myself he's trying to focus on our experiment, but I don't think that's the whole reason.

"Garrett, are you okay?"

He looks up, adjusting his safety glasses to see me better, then just shrugs.

"Are you mad at me?"

"No."

"Well, why so glum, chum?" I give him a cheesy smile.

"I don't know."

"Everything okay at home?"

"Yeah, I guess."

"How's the counseling stuff going?" I ask as I remember that he's still working through some issues, although he's been claiming he doesn't need any more help and really doesn't think he's gay.

"It's okay." He makes a face. "I told my counselor I don't need any more sessions, but she says she'll let me know when it's time to quit."

"That's probably good."

He rolls his eyes, then sort of nods.

"So are you concerned about your court appearance?" I know that comes up next week.

"Maybe."

Aha. Something about the flicker in his dark eyes tells me I might have hit pay dirt here. "Do you think they're going to prove you guilty?"

"Not really."

"But you're worried?"

He scowls, then looks back at the experiment. "I need to focus on this, Sam. Unless you want to take over."

"No, that's okay. But why don't we talk later."

He nods without saying anything.

Then I remember I have a task-force meeting after school. So I ask him if it's okay if I call him tonight or maybe meet him for coffee.

He brightens a little, and we agree to meet at seven at the Starbucks not too far from his house. Hopefully, Olivia will give me a ride.

"I have band practice this afternoon," she says as she takes me to the police station. "So I can't pick you up by five."

"I can call Mom and catch a ride with her." I mention meeting Garrett for coffee and ask Olivia if she wants to join us.

"I'd like to. But let me get back to you on that, okay?"

Then I get out, wave good-bye, and go into my first methamphetamine task-force meeting. I'm not that surprised to find I'm the only teenager here. Mostly it's cops, a few city officials, a doctor, and a couple of rehab counselors. Ebony is chairing the committee and handles the introductions. To my relief, she doesn't mention anything about my "gift" but instead describes my role with her as a "consultant from the teen sector," explaining how my dad used to be her partner and how I've been helpful in solving some cases that involved teens.

This first meeting is mostly educational. The experts share what they know about addiction, manufacturing of the drug, how it impacts the crime rate, and things like that. I listen carefully, like I think there might be an exam later, but it's somewhat redundant with the information in the packet Ebony gave me last week. Probably the best thing about this meeting is the reassurance that people are very concerned. And this group wants to do everything possible to educate our community about the problem and put a lid on it.

After the meeting, Ebony asks me to meet with her privately in her office. First she asks if I've read any of the book she gave me.

"As a matter of fact, I'm almost halfway through it," I tell her. "It's actually pretty interesting…and informative."

She nods. "Good."

"Did you talk to the chief?"

"I did."

"And?"

"He has agreed to a trial period, Sam. He asked me to put together some guidelines, which I did last night. And I've agreed to be responsible for your training."

"Really?" I feel excited now. "I really get to do this?"

"Yes." She hands me a large yellow envelope. "I want

you to read through this material, and we'll meet a couple times weekly to go over the basics."

"Cool."

"And you need to promise me that you'll be very careful, Samantha, that you will take this very seriously."

"Of course, I will." I nod. "You can trust me, Ebony."

"No risk taking, no playing hero."

"Absolutely."

Then she reaches into her desk drawer and pulls out a set of keys and grins. "And, we've decided to let you use a department car."

"A cruiser?" I tease, knowing full well they would never allow me to drive one of their prized black and whites. Still, I'm slightly shocked they're actually letting me use any of their cars. But I try to act natural.

She laughs. "Not quite."

Then I imagine a car like hers, a conservative-looking, dark gray Chevy sedan, and I hope I can appear appropriately grateful. I mean, who am I to complain about getting a set of wheels?

"I already talked to your mom about it," she says. "We needed her complete approval. Plus, she needed to sign the insurance papers since you're a juvenile."

"And she was okay with it?"

"She was happy about it."

"Cool."

"Want to see it?"

I nod. "Yeah, sure."

"I've got the insurance papers and some other agreement forms here," she says, "but maybe you'd like to actually see the car before you sign them."

Is she worried that if I don't like the car I won't sign the papers? I don't care how ugly the car is. I will like it. I will like it. I will like it. Ebony's guiding me down a hallway that leads out to the garage. I'm mentally preparing myself for my "new" car. I'm telling myself to smile and look excited when she shows it to me. I so don't want to offend her.

"You also get a parking spot down here," she says as we go down a stairwell. "But I don't think you should use it if you're really doing surveillance. You wouldn't want any of your peers to observe you pulling into the police-department garage. Might look suspicious."

"Good point."

She makes some more good points as we continue down to the garage. Finally she's quiet, and our footsteps echo through the underground garage as we walk past a row of shiny cruisers and then some of the dull-colored unmarked cars. Finally she stops in front of a lime green VW Bug that looks totally out of place. "Here you go." She hands me the set of keys.

"You're kidding?" I stare at the incredibly cute car. "Is this really it?"

"Yep."

"But...how?"

"The department confiscates vehicles occasionally," she explains, "from crime scenes and whatnot."

"You mean this was a criminal—"

"Don't worry. We traded a couple of the other vehicles for this one. The car is innocent."

I laugh as I run my hand over the hood. *"Wow!"*

"It's not new," she says, like I even care. "It's three years old, but it's in good shape. The department will provide your gas for any surveillance work. Other than that, you're on your own."

"Wow," I say again. "This is so awesome."

"So you approve?"

"I totally love it!" I'm so happy right now that I want to jump up and down and scream like a game-show contestant, but remembering we're in the police-department garage, I control myself. "So why did you pick a car like this?"

"Good question." She grins. "Well, besides the fact I thought you might like it, we were concerned about you driving a car that looked too official. This seemed like the sort of car a high-school girl would drive just for fun. And we want to protect your cover. This car will get attention, but not in a negative way."

"No one would ever think this was a cop car."

She nods. "Exactly. Now let's go sign those papers."

Thirty minutes later I am driving this adorable car through town and wearing the biggest smile ever. I so cannot believe it!

Nine

Mom is just pulling into the driveway when I get home. She parks in the garage, then comes back out to look at my car.

"It's cute, Samantha," she says after giving it the once-over. "I can't believe they did this for you."

"Well, they're only letting me *use* the car. It's not like they gave it to me."

"Be careful," she warns. "This is a small car. You need to be a cautious driver in it."

"It has air bags."

"Just don't use them."

"I'm trying to figure out how to explain this to my friends," I admit. "I mean, I don't want to lie, but I can't mention the connection to the department either."

"That is a problem, isn't it?" Her brow creases, and I know she's trying to come up with a solution.

"What if I say that *you* helped me get it," I say suddenly. "Since, in a way, you did. I mean, Ebony told me they had to have your approval before they got the car."

"That's true."

"So I never would've gotten it without you."

"Yes...I suppose that's right."

"Do you mind if I say that?"

"I think that's fine."

"Do you think Zach will be jealous?"

She considers this. "He shouldn't be. After all, I helped him get his first car too. And look where that ended up."

I nod, remembering how Zach ended up losing his car because of drugs. "Yeah, I guess he can't really complain."

So it's settled. I'll tell anyone who wants to know that Mom helped me get the car. To make it sound more realistic, I'll mention that I've been saving up, which is also true. I actually rehearse this line in my head a couple of times as I help Mom take some bags of groceries into the house. Just in case.

"Whose car?" Zach asks when he notices my green Bug in the driveway.

"Mine," I tell him as I put a gallon of milk in the fridge.

He looks puzzled. "Since when?"

"Since today."

"No way."

I nod. "Yeah. I've been saving for a while, and Mom helped me."

"Cool." He slaps me on the back. "My baby sister's got wheels. Now maybe I can bum a ride from you sometimes."

"Or you can get a job and get your own car," Mom says as she unloads groceries from a bag.

"I'm working on it," he says in a slightly grumpy tone. Then he grabs a can of soda and makes a hasty exit.

Mom lets out a loud sigh as she puts a box of cereal in the pantry. I can tell she's frustrated, and I'm not sure what I can say to encourage her. But I do know how she feels.

"It's like he's stuck," I finally say.

"Yes."

"I've even considered offering to go to an NA meeting with him. You know, just to get the wheels rolling."

She sort of laughs. "I don't think they like people to come who don't have addiction problems of their own."

"But I could offer him a ride. I know there's one tonight at the community center, and I promised to meet a friend for coffee."

Mom brightens. "Why don't you suggest this to Zach?"

And so I do, with Mom backing me. To our surprise, Zach agrees. "Yeah," he says. "I've been thinking I need to get back into this."

So I drop Zach at the community center and head over to Starbucks to meet Garrett. Olivia begged out because of homework, but she did promise to pray for our conversation after I told her I thought it might be serious.

"Whose car?" Garrett asks when I go inside the coffee shop. He's standing by the window, admiring my new wheels.

I grin at him. "Mine."

"Seriously?"

I nod. "Yep. I just got it today."

"I didn't know you were thinking about getting a car."

"Well, it was sort of sudden," I admit. "I've been saving, and my mom helped me…and the timing just seemed right."

"Did you get a good deal?"

"Oh yeah," I tell him. "Really good."

"Sweet."

We get our coffee and sit at a table by the window where I can keep an eye on my car. Then Garrett gets quiet.

"So, what's going on, Garrett? I know something's up."

He frowns and looks down at his cup.

"I'm your friend," I tell him. "Whatever it is, I think you know you can trust me."

"Yeah…" He looks up at me. "I do trust you, Sam."

"So tell me what's bugging you. Is it the court thing?"

"It's related."

I feel like I'm pulling teeth here, but I really do care about Garrett, so I persist. "Does it have to do with the drug test you wouldn't take?"

"Yeah…sort of."

I'm trying not to convey my shock, but suddenly I'm seriously worried that the Ziploc baggie in the backseat really might've been his after all. "Garrett, do you have a drug problem?"

He nods without speaking.

I brace myself. "Was that meth residue in the baggie from you?"

"No," he says quickly. "That wasn't mine. I swear it wasn't."

"So, you want to explain?"

He glances around almost as if he suspects we're being spied on. "It started about a year ago. I found an old prescription of my mom's in the medicine cabinet. It was for Effexor, an antidepressant, and since I was depressed, I started taking it. Then I actually managed to get the prescription refilled a couple of times before it expired. After that, I had to find other ways of getting my little happy pills."

"Illegal ways."

"Of course."

"Have you told your counselor about this?"

He shakes his head.

"Have you told anyone?"

He points at me.

"So you're still taking your little happy pills?"

"I have to. I need them."

"Where do you get them?"

"Here and there." He shrugs. "I have connections."

"Right…"

"That's why I couldn't take that drug test."

"Obviously." Suddenly I feel really uncomfortable. I mean, I work with the police, I'm on the drug task force, and I'm sitting here listening to compromising confessions from my friend. What am I supposed to do? I shoot up a quick prayer, asking God for some direction.

"I probably shouldn't have told you." Garrett is looking down at his coffee again, and I can tell he's feeling lousy.

"No, no…" I study him for a moment, considering all this guy has been through—an abusive dad, the fear that he was gay, his obsession with suicide, and this addiction problem. "I'm glad you told me, Garrett. They say the first step in recovery is admitting you have a problem."

He frowns. "How do you know about recovery?"

So I tell him a bit about Zach. I don't go into all the details but enough to help him understand that I know a little about this. I even tell him that Zach is still struggling and that I had to sort of rope him into going to a meeting tonight.

"Maybe I should go too."

I nod eagerly. "Yes, you really should."

He slumps slightly now.

"But even more than that, you need to get help from your counselor, Garrett. It's possible you really do have a chemical imbalance and need some form of treatment. I mean, there was the whole suicide thing…"

"Yeah, but I've heard that using antidepressants can lead to suicide, especially for teens."

"Really?"

He nods sadly. "You know me, Sam. I do my research."

"And knowing this, you continued to use them anyway?"

"That's the big problem with addiction. You do it, despite the risks, despite what it does to you. I know it doesn't really make sense. It's like you don't own it; it owns you."

"Do you want to quit?" I study his expression carefully now.

He looks back at me with somber eyes. "Yes."

I believe him. "Then you're going to need some help. I mean, besides me, although I'll do what I can. You need professional help."

"You really think I should tell my counselor?"

"I think it's a place to start."

"I really do want to be free of this," he admits. "It's stressful trying to get the pills…sometimes not even being sure if they're the real thing or a ripoff."

"Or what if they had something really harmful in them?" I suggest.

"I've considered that."

"Do you think you'll be able to tell your counselor, Garrett?"

He shrugs. "I meet with her tomorrow."

"How about if I drive you?" I offer. "And I could even come in with you if it would help. I mean, just while you told her about this. I wouldn't stay for your whole session or anything."

"Kind of an accountability thing?"

"Yes, to encourage you."

He smiles a little. "Okay."

"What time is your appointment?"

"Four."

"So, it's a date?"

He agrees, and I offer him a ride home in my new car.

"Beats walking," he says as we stand to leave.

Then I remember Zach. "I need to pick up my brother at the community center. His NA meeting. Do you mind?"

He laughs. "Hey, maybe it'll inspire me to go to the next meeting myself."

But when we get to the community center, I don't see Zach anywhere. We go inside, and although there are a few stragglers after the meeting, Zach doesn't seem to be around. And I am totally bummed by this.

"I wonder if he even went to the meeting," I say to Garrett as we get back in the car.

"Maybe he caught a ride with someone else."

"He could've called me." I feel angry as I start my car. Why is Zach acting like this? What is wrong with him? Doesn't he want to get well?

"Are you crying, Sam?"

I reach up, wipe my cheek, and nod. Realizing I'm not fit to drive, I turn off the engine and just sit there with both hands gripping the steering wheel. "I know it's stupid to take this, you know, so personally," I sob out. "But I really do love my brother…and I-I just want him to beat this thing. But it's like he's not…he's not even try-ing." Then I lean my head on the steering wheel and just cry.

Garrett reaches over and actually puts his hand on my shoulder now. "Drugs are seriously messed up, Sam."

I turn to look at him, surprised that he seems to be feeling sorry for me now. I just nod and wipe the tears from my face, trying to get control again.

"Sorry," I tell him.

"It's okay."

"I so wish there were no such thing as drugs. I hate how they mess people up. Good people too. Like you and Zach. It's just so wrong."

He shrugs. "Or just the human condition."

I nod. "Yeah, the human condition without God. People need God more than they need drugs. I wish everyone could see that."

"Maybe you should make a bumper sticker," he teases. "Instead of Hugs, Not Drugs, yours could say God, Not Drugs."

I restart my car. "Yeah, well, maybe I should. I mean, hugs are good and fine. But God's love and strength can get you through a whole lot more than a hug can."

Ten

The next day I decide to drive Olivia to school for a change. I don't give her any warning though. I just go over to her house about ten minutes before she'd normally leave and knock on the door.

"What're you doing here?" she asks.

"Picking you up."

"Huh?"

I nod over my shoulder to where my green Bug is parked in her driveway.

"Whose car?"

"Mine."

"Seriously?"

So I do my little spiel about how Mom helped me and how I'd been saving and the timing was just right.

"That is so cool, Sam. Let me grab my stuff and I'm ready."

It feels so great to be driving my own car. Okay, it's not really *my* car, but it's almost the same. And already I'm entertaining ideas of offering to buy it from the police department…someday.

"How'd it go with Garrett last night?"

Before I dropped Garrett at home, I told him that Olivia

really loves him too and has been praying for him, and he said it was okay to let her know about his "little problem." I try not to make it sound overwhelming, but even so, she is dismayed.

"I just wouldn't have thought he'd fall into something like that," she finally says.

"Because he's too smart?" I say in a slightly sarcastic tone.

She sighs loudly, then throws up her hands. "Oh, I don't know… I guess I really don't understand about this crud. Doing drugs, to me, is like taking a club and beating yourself over the head with it. I mean, I just don't get it."

I laugh. "That's because you're just so healthy. You should thank God for that, Olivia."

"Yeah, I guess. But for the grace of God that could be me, huh?"

"You never know."

"Well, it's just hard to imagine."

"It's not hard for me to imagine."

"That's because God gives you visions and things."

The image of Felicity in that vision flashes through my mind now, and I almost say something. But then I remember I never told Olivia about it. I didn't describe how it looked like Felicity was dead or how it seemed like drugs were involved. And if I'm going to succeed in my undercover investigating, I'll need to remain quiet. But I do tell Olivia about how Garrett said I could go to his counselor with him. "To help him get this out in the open," I say. "Kind of an accountability thing."

"Would you drop me off at Cameron's to practice first?"

"Sure. Two days in a row?"

"Yeah, we have a gig tomorrow night."

"What kind of gig?"

She frowns now. "Well, it's a party...but Cameron assured me it won't be anything like that last one." Then she looks hopefully at me. "You wouldn't want to come along, would you?"

Okay, I'd like to tell her to forget it. I mean, when I think about where we ended up after the last one, it seems crazy. But then I remember that I'm on a job now. I'm doing surveillance. Who knows what I might uncover at a Friday-night party? And so I agree.

Olivia laughs as I park my car away from the others. "Trying to protect your baby Bug?"

"You know how careless some high-school kids can be," I say sheepishly. "I don't want to get door dings the first time I drive it to school."

I have journalism second period and am dismayed to see that Felicity is absent today. Okay, it could just be a normal absence—she might have the flu or even be skipping—but because of that vision...well, I'm worried. I wish I knew her phone number, but I don't. Finally, at lunchtime, I decide to approach the only one I can think of who's actually her friend. Jack.

Naturally, Jack probably wouldn't be in the cafeteria with the seminormal people. But I know some of his hang-outs, and I decide to go look around. I clue Olivia in to my plans, but I tell her I need to do this alone.

"Just get me a salad." I hand her some money. "Hopefully, I'll be back in a few minutes."

"Should I tell Conrad what you're doing?"

I shrug. "Whatever."

Then I set out to find Jack. But I do not look forward

to speaking with this dude. The truth is, he creeps me out. And okay, I know God loves him. And I have been praying for him. But the idea of actually talking to him is unnerving.

After checking out a couple of his favorite haunts, I start to wonder if he's not here today either. Maybe they are skipping together. Maybe they're off getting high or making a drug deal. The thought of this makes me feel slightly sick. Then just as I'm about to give up, I spot Jack over by the west parking lot. He's with a couple of his friends. Kids that if I weren't a Christian, I would call losers. Losers. But God loves them. God loves them. This is what I tell myself as I walk toward them.

They stop talking when I'm about twenty feet from them. They're still smoking, and what they're smoking doesn't even look like cigarettes but probably weed. Oh, well. There are three guys, and they're all just staring at me with suspicious eyes. I feel like I'm in over my head, so I pray as I take a couple more steps. *God, help me.*

"Hey, Jack," I call out in a friendly tone. His brows pull together, and he glares at me. I can tell he doesn't want me around. I probably remind him of Olivia…and how she's part of the reason he's out of the band now.

"I just wanted to ask you something."

He growls a profanity, and a skinny blond guy hits him in the arm with his fist. "Lighten up, Jack."

"Yeah, man," says the other guy. "The lady just wants to talk to you."

"And she's cute," says the skinny blond.

"Thanks," I say with a forced smile. "I don't want to interrupt you guys, but I'm looking for Felicity."

Jack's eyes flicker with interest for a second, then he scowls. "Why?"

"She wasn't in journalism today, and I need to talk to her about something."

"What?"

"Just a project. Do you know where she is or how I can get hold of her?"

"Jack's been calling her all morning," says the blond guy. "The girl's not answering."

"Yeah," says the other guy. "Jack's getting nervous."

"She's probably dumping him," says the blond.

"Shut up, Garth!" snaps Jack.

"So you haven't seen her?" Okay, now I'm getting concerned, but I try to remain nonchalant. I can't let on that I'm worried about her.

Jack shakes his head and actually seems to soften some. "I haven't seen her since yesterday."

I think this could be my opportunity. "For what it's worth," I begin carefully, "I don't think Felicity is dumping Jack." I say this to the blond guy named Garth. "From what she's told me, Jack is her best friend. She seems to like him a lot."

"She told you that?" asks Jack.

"Yeah."

He nods now, and I see a trace of sadness in his eyes.

"I know she's been lonely since transferring here from Madison," I continue, thinking I should at least make myself a case. "I've been trying to get to know her. She seems pretty cool. And she's smart too."

"Yeah," he says, "she is."

"Do you think she might be sick?"

He just shrugs.

"Or maybe just skipping?" I add.

"Maybe."

"Well, could I get her phone number from you so I can tell her about this journalism project? We're supposed to have partners for it, and I wanted her to be mine." Okay, this isn't exactly true, and I'm feeling desperate as the image of an unconscious Felicity on that red sofa flashes through my head again.

"Yeah, I guess it's okay." Jack glances at his buddies, and they sort of nod their approval. "You got a pen?"

I quickly pull out a pen and a scrap of paper and write down what is obviously a cell phone number. "Sorry to bug you guys," I say as I slip it back into my bag.

"It's okay," says Jack.

"You want me to tell her to call you if I get hold of her?"

"Yeah, sure." Jack almost smiles but not quite. "That'd be cool."

Then I thank them for their time, and they almost seem to be sort of okay with me. Like I could almost be one of them. And I feel slightly stunned. Or maybe I'm experiencing a form of culture shock—I read about that in my humanities class last semester. As I walk away, I feel like I just visited another planet where I thought the inhabitants might kill me and eat me for lunch, but they turned out to be somewhat civilized instead.

I try Felicity's number a couple of times, but her phone and her voice mail are both turned off. Finally I give Ebony a call. I quickly remind her of the vision I had, even though I already told her about it on Wednesday. Then I add my concerns that Felicity is absent today.

"Do you think something has happened to Felicity," asks Ebony, "something that should be checked out by the police?"

I'm not sure how to respond. "Possibly," I finally say. "I mean, the vision I had didn't look good. But on the other hand, I was hoping Felicity could lead me to a dealer or something more significant."

"Let me look into it," she tells me. Then she takes down Felicity's cell-phone number. "I'll get this traced to a street address, then I'll let you know what I come up with."

"Thanks, Ebony. I mean, it might be nothing...at least I hope that's the case."

"But if Felicity *is* in danger, the most important thing is to help her."

After school I drop Olivia at band practice and take Garrett to his counselor where, after a quick introduction, I sit in while he confesses his addiction problem to her.

She nods and makes a note of something, then looks at me with a curious expression. "Is that why you're here?"

I feel sort of silly now, like maybe it wasn't really necessary or maybe I should just mind my own business. "I was just trying to give him some moral support, you know?"

She smiles at me. "Good for you. That's what friends are for."

Then I ask Garrett if he'd like me to wait for him in the lobby while he finishes his appointment, and he nods yes.

Ebony calls while I'm in the waiting area. She tracked down Felicity's address, which is on the other side of town. "I've learned a few things about her too," Ebony says in a somber tone.

"Anything I should know?"

"She was expelled from Madison."

"Do you know why?"

"No, apparently the police weren't involved, but I suspect it was drug related. Maybe it wasn't anything they could prove, and they decided to just let it go."

"Oh."

"But until this past year, she was a pretty good student."

"She does seem smart…but unhappy."

"Her parents divorced a couple of years ago. She's been living with her mom but, judging by the address, in a bad part of town. They must be having a hard time of it financially."

"That's too bad."

"Yeah…" Ebony sighs. "And if Felicity is using serious drugs, which seems likely, she's got to be getting money for that somehow. It's not cheap to support an addiction like that."

"Where do you think she'd get money?"

"The obvious possibilities are working for a dealer or prostitution…or both."

Now this doesn't really surprise me, and yet it makes me sad. Incredibly sad.

"I know it's hard to hear that, Samantha. But these are the facts."

"I just feel so sorry for her. What a horrible way to live."

"Well, hopefully you'll be able to help her. Maybe even prevent her from something much worse. God gave you that vision for a reason."

"Yes," I say with a little more enthusiasm. Then Ebony gives me Felicity's address, just in case I think I should stop by, although I'm not sure what I'd say to her if I found her there. How would I explain how I knew where she lived or why I'd come? That journalism story might've worked for Jack, but Felicity is actually in my journalism class. She would know it wasn't true.

Anyway, I'll need God's direction before I show up uninvited on anyone's doorstep. After I hang up with Ebony, I really pray for Felicity. I pray for God to keep her safe for the time being and for her somehow to get the help she needs. Most of all, I pray she discovers that only God has the answers for her life. *God, not drugs.* Yeah, maybe I will make a bumper sticker.

ow did that go?" I ask Garrett after his counseling session. We're back in my car, and I
don't like to be too nosy, but I do care. I want Garrett to
get free of this thing.

"Okay…"

"Good. So what's next then?"

"Huh?"

"You know," I say, "what's the next step to help you
recover?"

"Oh…she referred me to a doctor. And she told me
that I need to inform my foster parents about my problem."

I can tell he's not comfortable with this. "Are you worried about how they might react?"

He nods. "They're nice people and all, but they're really
into their church and living a good clean life, you know?
It might really mess things up when they find out the
truth about me."

"Or it might not."

He frowns, and I can tell he's not convinced. "Would it
help if I was with you when you told them?"

He shrugs. "I don't know…"

"I mean, it's not like I think someone needs to hold

your hand, Garrett. But you've been through some pretty hard things this past year, and I can understand the need to have someone in your court."

"Yeah, I guess it would be good."

I glance at the clock on my dashboard. "I don't need to pick up Olivia for another hour. Do you think your foster parents are home?"

"Marsha probably is."

"Why don't we go see?" His foster mom, Marsha Landrum, works from her home. I've only met her once, but she seems pretty nice. Okay, maybe a little conservative but kind.

Garrett is really quiet as I drive across town. I wish I could think of something to say that would encourage him, but right now I'm worried about Felicity. I hope she's okay. I turn on the radio to fill in the quiet space as I silently pray for her, and in a few minutes we are walking up to the door of Garrett's house.

"Hello," Marsha calls out as she comes around the side of the house. She has on black rubber boots and is carrying a hoe in one hand. "Just doing some weeding. All that rain has brought out the weeds." She pauses in front of us, pushes a strand of gray hair out of her eyes, and smiles warmly.

"We wanted to talk to you," I begin. Garrett is looking down at his feet with a tightly clamped jaw. I just hope he can do this.

"Sure," she says as she peels off her garden gloves, then glances at Garrett. "Is anything wrong?"

He still isn't talking, and I'm suddenly wondering if this is a mistake. "Maybe we should go inside."

"Of course." Marsha heads up to the porch. Kicking off her muddy boots, she opens the door and waves us in. She offers us something to drink, but I decline, and Garrett sits down in a dejected sort of way. It's going to be up to me to break the ice.

"We just got back from Garrett's counseling appointment," I begin, "and his counselor thought that—"

"I can do this," he says quickly. "I need to tell you that I have a problem..." He looks directly at Marsha now. "And when you hear what it is, you may decide you don't want to have me in your home."

I can see a trace of alarm in her eyes, and I wonder what she might be imagining. Does she think he's a psycho, a killer, a child abuser? Poor Garrett. But he tells her the same story he told me, and finally he's done.

"Oh..." She folds her hands in her lap. "Well, that's not so terrible, Garrett. Were you worried about telling us?"

He looks surprised. "Yeah...sort of."

She smiles. "Maybe it's my turn to tell you something about me." She takes a deep breath and sits up straighter. "I'm sure you assume that my life has been pretty normal." She sort of laughs. "But what you don't know is that I had a similar problem. Oh, it was years ago, back after my last child was born in the midseventies. I had my wisdom teeth removed. No big deal, but the doctor prescribed pain pills, and I got hooked."

"Hooked?" Garrett looks doubtful.

She nods. "Yes. I became addicted. I started making up reasons for getting my prescription renewed. I told the doctor that I'd sprained my neck lifting the baby. The next time it was something else. Finally he questioned my need for these pills, and I switched doctors. Within the course of three years, I must've seen a dozen different doctors, getting prescriptions from all of them. I can barely remember those years." She sadly shakes her head. "My children were young and needed me, and although I was there… I really wasn't."

Now Garrett looks truly surprised. "What happened?"

"I finally came to the end of my rope and completely fell apart. I had a nervous breakdown and was hospitalized for a couple of weeks. Those were the darkest, hardest, longest, most depressing two weeks of my life. I didn't think I'd ever survive it."

"Wow," I say. "How did you?"

"I found God. I was in the bottom of a deep, black pit, and God reached down and took my hand."

"That is so cool." I glance over at Garrett, curious to see his response. She seems to still have his attention.

"It still took time and work to recover," she admits. "I had been doing some very heavy medicating." She looks directly at Garrett. "Probably even worse than what you've been doing. But I never could've escaped my addiction without God's help."

"I don't think it's a coincidence that Garrett ended up in your home," I tell her. "It's so great that you understand this."

She nods. "Yes, I definitely do."

I look at my watch and stand. "Well, I need to go pick up my friend now." I glance at Garrett, and he's staring at Marsha like he's still trying to absorb what she just told him.

"See ya tomorrow, Garrett."

"Thanks, Sam." He smiles at me now, and I have a

strong feeling that he's going to be okay. He's going to get through this. God has His hands on that boy.

"Yes," Marsha says with moist eyes. "Thanks for helping us share our stories today. It'll be a new beginning for everyone."

When I get to Cameron's house, the band members are standing outside by the garage, just talking. I pull up and get out, feeling slightly out of place as I go over and join them.

"Hey," says Olivia. "I was about to call you. We quit a little early."

"Because we sounded so hot," brags Cameron. "We figured, why mess with a good thing?"

"So what did you do about your missing bass player?" I ask. The truth is, I'm feeling just a little sorry for Jack today. He lost his place in the band, and his girlfriend is missing.

"Kyle plays bass too," says Olivia. "So I'm doing keyboard for now, and he's doing bass."

"But that's just a temporary fix," says Cameron, "until we find another bass player. You know anyone?"

"Sorry."

"I told them I'd talk to Maxwell Price," says Olivia.

"Maxwell?" I give her a curious look, which she returns with a warning glance.

"Yes," she says quickly. "He plays a lot of instruments, but he's really good on bass. Haven't you heard him?"

I nod. Of course I've heard him. He plays in our church's worship band every Sunday. But he's not exactly a Stewed Oysters kind of guy. He goes to Madison High and is one of the most evangelistic people I know. Not that I have a problem with people telling others about Jesus.

I don't. But sometimes it seems like Maxwell Price is keeping a head count—like he thinks there'll be a special reward in heaven for how many people he coerces into the faith. Okay, that's not fair, but I do question his methods sometimes. And I can't believe Olivia would consider asking him to join the Oysters. Even so, I keep my mouth shut.

The group breaks up, and Olivia and I get into my car where I question her judgment. "Maxwell Price?"

She laughs. "Wouldn't it be hilarious?"

"I suppose, but it could get ugly too."

"It was just an idea. I doubt Maxwell would even agree." She leans back and sighs. "Hey, I like this new setup, being chauffeured around by you for a change."

"It's about time." Then I give her the latest on Garrett, and she claps her hands and cheers. "That's awesome, Sam!"

"I know. I couldn't believe his foster mom. I mean, she looks like this old fuddy-duddy lady, and she was so totally cool. It was a real God-thing."

"Well, I've really been praying for that boy. God's not done with him yet."

"Hopefully, God's not done with any of us, Olivia."

"Amen!" Then she cranks up my CD player, and we both start singing along. Of course, her singing actually sounds good. But at least I have enthusiasm.

"I found out a little more about tomorrow night's gig," she tells me when we get to her house. "It's a birthday party too."

I let out a groan.

"But not a sweet sixteen. This is for a couple of guys who go to Madison. They're twins, and they're turning eighteen. It's a surprise party their parents are giving. Cameron assured me it wouldn't be crazy."

"Yeah, right. How can he promise anything?"

"I know. So I told him that if I see any alcohol or drugs, I'm outta there. And I plan to tell the parents the same thing."

"Seriously?"

"Yep."

"Good for you."

After I drop off Olivia, I try Felicity's number again, but it's just the same. No answer, no messaging service. This does not seem normal. I decide just to drive by where Felicity lives. I won't stop. I won't even slow down. I just want to see it for myself.

Ebony is right about the neighborhood. It's really bad. The houses are old and run-down and small. Some of them even have old furniture piled around, like someone just decided to throw everything out. The yards are mostly patches of weeds and junk. And the cars parked here and there don't look like they could even run. Very sad. I see the tiny house where Felicity lives—a small white one with peeling paint, just as bad as the rest. I cannot even imagine going up there and knocking on the door. Seriously, this looks like the kind of neighborhood where a person could get shot.

I keep on driving. But as I drive, I ask God to specifically show me what I need to do about Felicity. "You gave me that vision," I remind Him. Like God needs a reminder. "Please show me why. What can I do?"

Then I know I need to just trust Him. And wait.

The next day, Friday, Felicity is absent again. And at noon, it's Jack who approaches me. I force a tiny smile for him, and he looks slightly less threatening than usual. This is a guy with those dark, slightly scary looks—like *don't mess with me, man.* But the more I get to know him, the less intimidating he seems.

"Did you get hold of Felicity?" he asks.

"No. I tried a bunch of times. Nothing."

He nods with a creased brow. "Me too."

I study his dark eyes for a moment. He seems sad. "Do you think she's okay, Jack?"

He looks surprised by my question, but I decide to pursue this a bit more. "I mean, I know she's into some stuff…" I glance around like I don't want anyone to hear us, but we're standing off by ourselves outside the cafeteria. "That could be dangerous, you know?" I look at him, and he nods, just barely. "And anyway, I guess I'm worried that something could've happened to her. I was wishing I had her mom's phone number."

"They don't have a phone in the house," he says. "And her mom just has one of those cheap cell phones for emergencies only."

"Have you met her mom?"

"Sort of." He shrugs. "I saw her. She's not much of a mom."

I want to ask him what he means by this, but I don't want to seem too nosy. I don't want to make him suspicious. "That's too bad."

"Yeah. Felicity says she pretty much takes care of herself. She can't count on her parents for anything."

"Does she have a job?"

He scowls, and I almost expect him to tell me to butt out. Then he mutters, "Sort of."

"Well, it's gotta be hard. I just hope she's okay."

"I stopped by her house this morning," he says. "Knocked on her door, but it was just like yesterday… Nobody answered."

I nod. "Well, if you hear anything or if there's anything I can do, let me know. I really do care about her."

"Thanks." Then he walks away.

Once again I'm stunned. Not that Jack talked to me— I recovered from that one yesterday. But I'm shocked that he almost seems to trust me. That is totally unexpected. But even as I think this, I feel guilty. I can't imagine what Jack would do if he knew I was working with the police. He'd probably assume I was a narc and was out to get both him and Felicity. And who knows how he would react to that. I mean, I've seen that guy when he's mad, and I think he may have a real anger problem. Okay, this is a truly frightening thought.

Suddenly I realize I need to be very careful. I need to rely on God more than ever just now. I seriously need Him to guide my steps. This is not a game.

I invited Garrett to come with us tonight," Olivia informs me when I pick her up. "But he turned me down because he was doing something with his foster parents. He also told me that his foster parents and his counselor are talking to the DA about some kind of plea bargain for him."

"That makes it sound like he's guilty," I point out.

"*Plea bargain* might be the wrong term. But he's going to exchange evidence about his own sources in order to be excused from going to trial. He may get stuck with some community service."

"That should be a relief. I know that whole trial thing's been hanging over his head."

"He said that it sounds like everyone's pretty convinced it was a plant in my car and that it had nothing to do with the three of us."

"Yeah, Ebony mentioned something like that to me this week."

"So things are looking up for old Garrett."

"That's cool," I say as I slow down for a light that's still green. I'm being extra careful with my "new" car. "And it's cool that he wants to get better acquainted with his foster family. His mom seems really sweet."

"Yeah. I think he's seeing them in a whole new light now."

"And I'm sure they weren't too excited about the possibility of him going to another party that could get busted." I kind of laugh, although I don't really think it's funny.

"Hopefully, that won't be the case. And if it is, we're like so outta there, Sam. I mean it."

"I'm with ya."

This time we don't do any back-alley parking. I leave my bright green car right in front of the well-lit house, where it's easily observable and where we can make a fast getaway if necessary. I also double-check to make sure my car is securely locked. I am taking no chances.

Fortunately, tonight's celebration looks like it'll be a lot tamer than that crazy sweet-sixteen party. It turns out that the family is Hindu, and entering their house feels like a minitrip to India. Throughout their home, I see ornately carved furniture, exotic fabrics, large sculptures, and colorful carpets. We meet Dr. and Mrs. Hassan, who politely introduce us to the birthday boys, Ajay and Vijay. These guys both seem pretty shy and slightly embarrassed by all this attention, but they start to loosen up when the band begins to play.

Their mother is wearing a sari of beautiful orange silk along with some expensive-looking jewelry. She and her husband actually dance to one of the slower songs, and I feel fairly certain these parents will be sticking around tonight.

Because it's an unseasonably warm evening with no rain, the party extends into the backyard, where small lanterns and strings of lights are everywhere. A canvas, tentlike awning is set up near the pool to protect the food tables. And for the first couple of hours, everything seems fun and lively, but not out of control. It seems that Ajay and Vijay are actually having a good time. I even take turns dancing with both of them.

It's about ten when I notice that the party is getting a lot more crowded and noisy. And the new faces are a little rougher looking, kids who don't exactly appear to be friends of the birthday boys. Ajay and Vijay are polite to the newcomers, but I can tell they're unsure what to do. I look around for the elder Hassans. They were just here a few minutes ago, and I'm sure they haven't left the premises, but I also suspect they're unaware of the party crashers.

I also notice that some of the recent arrivals have obviously been drinking and appear to be trying to turn this into a much wilder party. Voices grow loud, and kids act careless and crazy—the way people sometimes think it's okay to be when they're in someone else's home. The idea of things getting out of hand and ruining the Hassans' party or any of their lovely things is disturbing, so feeling a lot like a real cop, I set off in search of the parents. My hope is to give them a quick heads-up before it's too late.

I look for them out in the backyard without success, and just as I emerge from the food tent, I notice a girl standing by the swimming pool. I can't believe it—it's Felicity! She's okay! I try not to appear overly excited as I hurry over to speak to her. "Hey, Felicity," I say calmly. "What're you doing here?"

She shrugs. "Oh, I know Ajay and Vijay from my old school." She glances over her shoulder in a way that makes me wonder if she's actually a crasher too.

"I missed you in journalism class these past couple of days..."

"Jack told me you've been asking about me." She narrows her eyes now. *"Why exactly?"*

"Just because I missed you," I say lightly, even though it is redundant.

"Yeah, but Jack said you were *really* worried about me. I don't get that, Samantha. It's not like we're best friends or anything. What's up with that?"

Wanting to ward off her suspicion, I make a sheepish little smile and try to come up with a response before this goes totally sideways on me. "Well, it's weird, really," I say, deciding that honesty might be my best approach, although I obviously can't tell her everything. "Do you ever get a feeling about something—kind of like an intuition?"

She studies me warily, then slowly nods. "Yeah, that's happened to me before. Why?"

"Well, that happens to me a lot. And that day you weren't in journalism, I was thinking about you, and I just got this really uncomfortable feeling inside, an intuition that something was wrong. Enough that I got pretty worried about you."

She frowns. "Really?"

"Yeah. That's why I asked Jack about you."

"He said it was because of some journalism project."

"That wasn't exactly right. Mostly I just wanted to make sure you were okay." I smile at her. "And it looks like you are."

"Yeah, I guess."

Now I'm slightly perplexed. "Still, it does make me wonder..."

"What?"

"Well, when I get those feelings, they're usually right."

"Really?" She looks pretty skeptical now.

"Yeah." Okay, I'm not sure how deep I want to get into this. It could backfire on me. Still, if her safety or life is on the line…

"So what's your point?" she asks impatiently.

"Maybe that feeling I had is supposed to be a warning to you."

"A warning for what?"

"You know, like maybe you could be in some kind of danger."

"Yeah, right." She scowls. "What about life *isn't* dangerous?"

I shrug, unsure how to respond.

"Is that it then?" she asks in an irritated tone. "Like I'm supposed to take your random little warning seriously? Get real."

"I know it sounds pretty vague, but I guess if you're involved in anything that could…well, you know, be dangerous…maybe you need to watch out and be more careful."

Now she looks downright mad. "Is that some kind of threat?"

I hold up my hands as if to proclaim innocence. "No, of course not, Felicity. It's just that I thought we were friends. And I was honestly worried about you, and I felt like I should warn—"

"What's going on?" Jack demands from behind me, like he appeared out of nowhere. I hope he didn't see me jump or the fear in my eyes.

"Samantha is telling me this lame story," Felicity relays

to him in a sarcastic tone. "Like I'm in some sort of horrible danger."

"What kind of danger?" Jack frowns at me.

"I don't know exactly... I just had this feeling about her. I told Felicity that I get these intuitions sometimes, and I had one about her."

"And she starts telling me that I need to watch out so I don't get hurt." Felicity rolls her eyes.

But Jack peers closely at her now. "And what do you think?"

She laughs. "I think Samantha is full of it."

I force myself to laugh too. "Yeah, I get that a lot." Then I look directly into her eyes. "And no problem, you can think I'm crazy if you want. But seriously, if I didn't like you and if I didn't consider you my friend, I wouldn't have bothered to tell you this. Just take it for what it's worth. Okay?"

Her eyes soften a little. "Yeah, well, okay. It's just a little freaky."

"I know."

"The beverages at this party aren't much," Jack tells Felicity.

I nod. "Yeah, I think the parents are pretty conservative, and I know for a fact they won't tolerate any alcohol here."

"Maybe we should just go," says Jack.

"Yeah," says Felicity. "I heard there's a good party over on Oak Street tonight. Wanna check it out?"

"Let's get some food first." Jack nods toward the tent.

"Good to see you guys," I say, thinking I better make my escape. "I'm glad you're okay, Felicity."

She makes a smirky face. "Yeah, but I better watch out, huh?"

I shrug. "Just be safe, okay?"

She throws back her head and laughs loudly. Then Jack grabs her by the arm, and they head off to plunder the food that's left in the tent. Although I happen to know it's already picked over by now.

Okay, it's times like this that I sort of question myself. I mean, what am I doing giving warnings to someone like Felicity? Telling her about my "intuitions"? Acting like I know what's best for everybody? Like I think I'm the security guard, the safety patrol, the hall monitor? And yet God has given me this gift. I know I have this calling. How can I pretend it's not real?

I silently pray for wisdom and strength as I continue my search for the Hassans. And as I walk through the house, I see that the partyers have gotten even wilder. Ajay is standing near the stairs looking very uncomfortable, and Olivia is singing right now but giving me *the look*—like maybe we should split. I nod to her, hoping to assure her I'm okay, at least for the moment.

I find Mrs. Hassan back in the kitchen busily putting some things away. "I don't mean to intrude," I say in a quiet voice, "but I think some uninvited guests have come to your party."

She nods and frowns. "Yes, Vijay just told me this."

"And I think some have alcohol."

"Oh dear."

"I just wanted to let you know. You see, my friend Olivia, the girl in the band, has made it clear she won't play for parties where teens are drinking alcohol."

"Yes. That's understandable. I must inform Neri of this development. Thank you for telling me."

To my surprise, and probably everyone else's, Dr. Hassan loudly claps his hands and asks the band to stop playing so he can make an announcement.

"There is some misunderstanding here." He speaks in a loud but polite voice. "It has come to my attention that some of you were not invited to this party, and some of you teenagers have been imbibing alcohol. I ask you please to excuse yourselves from these premises before I am forced to call the authorities for police assistance." He pauses and looks at the crowd. "My apologies to our legitimate guests. Please remain and enjoy our hospitality until midnight." He smiles now. "Thank you very much."

Then almost as quickly as they came, the intruders trickle out. And after about fifteen minutes, the party is back to what it was before. I'm impressed with parents who really do care and who are willing to do the responsible thing, even if some kids think it's uncool. To me it's refreshing.

"You were out pretty late," Mom says to me when I finally get home. It's after midnight, and I explain about Olivia's gig and how I gave her a ride.

"Did you just get home too?" I ask, noticing that she's still wearing what she had on when she went out with Steven.

She smiles. "We went out dancing after the movie."

"Did you have fun?"

She nods, then looks at the clock. "But if we're getting up early to go skiing tomorrow, we'd better hit the hay."

"Is Zach home?"

She frowns. "Not yet."

"Oh…"

Then she shrugs. "Nothing we can do about that, Samantha."

"I guess."

But there is something I can do—pray for my brother. As I dig through my closet to find some ski gear for tomorrow, I pray that God will get Zach's attention and help him get back on track.

I smell smoke. But when I look around me, all I see is snow. Not crisp white snow like on a Christmas card, but snow that's been trampled and is dirty and dingy. And because it's getting dusky out, the shadows from pine trees are making it seem even darker, sort of a gray blue color that feels sinister and unclean and frightening.

Among the footprints, one particular set of prints catches my attention. They appear to have been made by tennis shoes, and for some unexplainable reason I know that the shoes were Adidas. Then without really considering what I'm doing or why, I follow these prints.

They lead in the direction of the smoke, and after walking about fifty yards, I notice a small wooden structure tucked into some trees up ahead. This is the source of the smoke and fire, and it's not a good fire. The smoke isn't curling out of the stone chimney on the roof but is escaping through cracks and crevices around the windows and doors. I see flickering yellow light dancing in the windows and reflecting out onto the snow. This out-of-control fire is devouring everything within the cabin, yet no one seems to be around or aware of what's going on.

I instinctively reach for my bag to get my cell phone to

call 911, but that's when I realize not only do I *not* have my bag and phone with me, but I am in my pajamas and barefoot! No wonder my feet are freezing.

Worried that someone might be in danger, I hurry toward the cabin, still following those same tennis-shoe footprints, which lead directly to the front door. I hop as I go, trying to protect my frostbitten feet from the icy surface of the snow.

The wooden structure is completely engulfed now. Bright orange flames, like an enormous bonfire someone forgot to tend, explode through the roof and leap into the darkening sky. I have to step back to keep the heat from burning my face.

I notice a stump nearby, like one that's been used to chop firewood on. So I go over and sit down on it and actually lift up my feet and face them toward the burning house, hoping to warm them.

Maybe something good will come from this strange fire. There's obviously nothing I can do to stop it, and as far as I can see, no one is in danger. But as I sit there, I notice this dark liquid trail cutting through the surface of the snow and trickling toward me. Thinking it's something leaking from the house, I follow it with my eyes. But what I see at the source of this trail is alarming.

I dash over to get a better look. There, only a few feet from the burning house, lying facedown in the snow, is a man. He's been shot, perhaps several times, and a dark pool of blood is staining the snow all around him. He has on a Gap denim jacket and white Adidas tennis shoes. And that's when it hits me.

Zach has those exact same shoes and jacket!

My hand flies up to my mouth as I shriek out his name. "Zach!"

Then I wake up. I am still shaking from the dream, and tears are streaming down my face. My feet are uncovered and are clammy and cold, and I am shivering. I pull my comforter closer around me and consider my dream.

"What does it mean, God?" I whisper. "I know it's a warning, but what does it mean?"

I get out of bed, and with my comforter still draped around me like a fluffy cape, I tiptoe out into the hallway and stealthily make my way to Zach's bedroom door. It's barely cracked open but enough that I can hear my brother quietly snoring. I let out a small sigh.

He's okay. At least for now.

'm surprised you made it up this morning," Mom tells Zach as we load things into the back of her car. Steven decided we should take her car today since his is too small for four people and ski stuff. Plus her Volvo already has a ski rack. My dad put it on about a year before he died. No one has even considered taking it off. It makes me sad to look at it. I try not to think that it should be my dad adjusting it right now. It should be his hands fastening the skis and poles securely. How much different would our lives be if that were the case? Yet I know there's no going back. And I know that God is bigger than all this. Somehow He must be able to sort this out too.

I'm being quiet as I sit in the backseat of the car, but Mom and Steven make up for it as they discuss the latest news—a stock-market slump that is impacting his job and budget cuts at her work, which mean more employee layoffs.

"I think they're trying to see who can win the pity prize today," Zach whispers to me, then laughs.

I nod and attempt a lame-sounding laugh. "Yeah. Wanna compete with them?"

He shrugs. "Well, I'm currently broke, jobless, fresh

out of rehab with absolutely no direction for my life. Some people think I'm a loser. How's that for starters?"

"What are you saying back there?" Mom turns around from the passenger seat and stares at us. (She asked Steven to drive since she doesn't like driving on snow.)

"We thought you were competing for the best sob stories," Zach explains. "I'm sure you'd all agree that I can win that one."

"Oh, Zach." Mom shakes her head. "If you'd only just try harder, I'm sure you could find work."

"Yeah, right," he says. "I mean, you two are up there complaining about the economy and job cuts, and now you act like getting a job is a piece of cake."

"I didn't say it was a piece of cake." She frowns. "I simply said you need to try harder."

"Sometimes there are people, especially job interviewers, who can read you, Zach," says Steven. "They can tell if you feel negatively about yourself. They catch those vibes and end up feeling the same way."

Zach gets a very dark look on his face, and I'm worried he's going to say something mean. We're only thirty minutes from home, not even halfway there yet, and this trip could go totally sideways. But Zach keeps his mouth shut. He just folds his arms across his chest and turns and looks out the side window. Still, I can tell he's ticked.

"I'm not telling you what to do, man," Steven says in a semiapologetic tone. He must suspect that Zach's not exactly swallowing this "fatherly" advice. "But sometimes we need to examine the bigger picture and learn from our mistakes, you know?"

"Yeah, whatever."

Okay, I know it's time for an intervention or our ski trip is going to be over before we even hit the highway, but all I can think about is last night's dream—Zach facedown in the snow. *Dear God, help me.*

"Speaking of learning from our mistakes," I begin suddenly. Then I tell them about last night's party, how it was crashed and how well the Hassans handled it. I can tell Zach's not impressed. In fact, he probably thinks I'm a big wet blanket since he'd be one of the kids who would want to party hearty. But Mom seems relieved.

"So that's why I didn't get a call from the jail last night," she teases.

"Yeah, but Olivia and I were ready to walk if we needed to. No way were we going to get stuck in something like that again."

Zach actually rolls his eyes at me now. But I can tell he's slightly relieved to have the spotlight off him. And Mom seems to get that Steven crossed over a line in his minilecture. I mean, there's no doubt that Zach needs someone to set him straight. But I just don't think Steven's the guy to do it. Anyway, Mom keeps the conversation light and mostly between Steven and her. Zach goes to sleep, or pretends to go to sleep. And I sit there and pray, asking God to lead me today.

For some reason—maybe the snow—I think last night's dream has something to do with today. And I don't plan to let Zach out of my sight. Okay, that's not going to be easy since last time we went snowboarding, he mostly left me in the dust, or the powder. But somehow I need to make him stick with me today. And who knows, maybe we'll even have a significant conversation.

But later when I attempt to bring up the subject of NA meetings and his mentor and working his recovery program, I am shut down.

"I am working my recovery program," he insists just seconds before we jump off the lift. "But it's *my* program, Sam. Not yours. Not Mom's. And for sure, it's not Steven's. You guys just all need to butt out and let me do this on my own. I mean, if there's one thing I learned in Washington, it's that it's up to me whether I succeed or not."

And then we're off the chair, and Zach tears down the mountain at breakneck speed. There's no way I can keep up. Not only that, but this run is way beyond my expertise. It takes me about thirty minutes to get down, and I'm pretty surprised that Zach is actually waiting for me when I get there.

"Sorry, Sis. I didn't mean to bite your head off up there."

I'm still slightly out of breath. "That's okay. I guess I shouldn't keep bugging you. It's just that I care."

He nods. "I know you do." Then he smiles, and it's one of those great Zach smiles that can disarm anyone, even a little sister. "And I'm glad you do. But you have to trust me, okay?"

"Okay."

"And you still want to ride with me?"

I say that I do, but I'm really not so sure. "Maybe an easier run this time?"

He agrees. And we take a couple of lower-level rides, but I can tell he's getting bored. So I try to do it his way. But by noon, I realize that keeping up with Zach on the slopes isn't just impossible; it's dangerous and stupid. After a nasty fall where I actually think I've broken a bone or sprained my knee, I give up on the hard runs. I do a couple more easy ones, just to make sure I'm not seriously injured, and then I retreat to the lodge, where I buy a soda and find a discarded *People* magazine that entertains me for the next hour.

"What are you doing in here all by yourself?" Steven asks as he sits in one of the big easy chairs across from me.

I point to my sore knee and describe my little wreck. "It was a total yard sale," I admit at the end of my saga. "I almost expected someone to make an offer on my pink ski hat since it was like twenty feet above me on the slope."

He laughs. "That's too bad. But your knee's feeling better now?"

"Yeah, I think it's okay. Where's Mom?"

"I'm not sure. She and I parted ways so I could do some more challenging runs, but we planned to meet here at three."

"Well, it's not quite three yet."

He nods, then frowns. "I think I put my foot in my mouth with your brother this morning."

"That's not too difficult to do."

"Still, I'd hoped today would be a breakthrough for us. I had actually imagined skiing with him—well, he'd be riding and I'd be skiing. I thought we'd have some nice little chats going up the lifts." He sighs. "I must've been slightly delusional or watched one too many episodes of *The Brady Bunch*."

"You really watch that?"

He looks slightly sheepish. "Sometimes."

This makes me laugh. "Well, Zach's still got stuff to deal with. You shouldn't take it too personally." I don't go into detail about how I got shut down today too. After all, Zach did apologize later.

"Yeah, I realize that. But I thought maybe I could help."

I consider this. "You know…if you want to help, it'd probably be better if you didn't try to sound too much like a parent. I mean, we had a dad, and he was cool. But Zach is twenty now. Even if he doesn't act like an adult, well, he sort of is. And I just don't think he's ready to have someone step into a father role."

Steven seems to chew on this and finally smiles. "I think you're right, Samantha. I probably overstepped my bounds."

His comments make me curious, and since Mom's not around, I decide to ask. "So, are you getting serious about my mom?"

Now he looks a little uncomfortable, but then he sits up straighter. "I don't know how you define *serious*. But I really do like your mother. And I think she likes me."

Okay, now I want to ask if his intentions are honorable. Really, those are the words that go through my head. But of course, I can't say that. "Are you guys exclusive then?"

He kind of shrugs. "Well, we haven't really defined our relationship. But I can say that I'm not dating anyone else."

"Oh…" Then I see Mom coming our way. I'm surprised at how young she looks with her flushed cheeks and messy hair. And she's smiling.

She flops down in the big armchair next to Steven and lets out a happy sigh. "I don't know when I've had such a fun day." She actually giggles now. "I mean, I've only been on the easy slopes, and I'm being really careful since it's the first time I've been on skis in years. But it feels so great to be up here. It reminds me of being a girl."

"Cool," I say, but probably not with as much enthusiasm as she'd like. I really am happy for her, but at the same time, I'm suddenly worried about Zach.

I'm thinking about that dream again and how he looked, lying facedown in the snow. Although I'm trying to convince myself it's not related to today. Or maybe I'm just in some kind of denial. But even so, it's not dusk here yet, and we'll be on our way home before that. And besides trampled snow and pine trees, I haven't seen a thing that resembles anything from my dream. Not any small cabin-like structures, not one whiff of smoke.

Okay, I realize my dream could have been a metaphor for something else. I do get dreams like that occasionally. But even that doesn't really make much sense. Well, other than the implication that Zach is in danger. And I don't really like to think about that.

Mom looks at her watch now. "I told Zach we'd be leaving at three thirty so we can avoid the end-of-the-day traffic jam out of here. Have you guys seen him anywhere?"

I admit to her that it's been almost two hours now, and Steven hasn't seen him since lunch. "Well, I told him to meet us here." Mom frowns. "But I wish I'd given him my cell phone."

"He doesn't have his own cell phone?" asks Steven.

"He doesn't even have his *own job*," she says in a slightly irritated tone.

His brows shoot up, and I suspect she stepped on his toes.

"Sorry, Steven. I didn't mean to tear into you like that.

It's certainly not your fault if my son makes us late." She gives him a little smile. "I don't want to sound ungrateful. It was so sweet of you to treat us to this incredible day. I just don't want anything to spoil it. Especially Zach."

"It's okay, Beth. I know some things can be trying for a mom."

She nods. "Yeah, it's not easy."

I wonder how much she's told him about my brother. And I'm not sure how I'd feel about it either way. I mean, it's not like Zach has exactly kept his mistakes top secret, and Steven is fully aware of his stint in rehab. I'm just not sure if he's aware that Zach might be failing now. And even though it feels slightly hopeless to me, especially after last night's dream that I assume is drug related, I still desperately want Zach to beat his addiction. I so want our family to move past this drug demon that my brother has introduced into our lives.

Fourteen

S o much for beating the traffic," Mom says as the parking lot starts getting jammed with SUVs and other vehicles, all trying to get in and out of here at the same time. The day skiing has finished up now, and night skiing will begin soon. Our day passes expired an hour ago. It's now close to five.

"Even if Zach took one last lift up at four, he should be down by now." Steven looks once again at his watch. I can tell he's getting impatient.

"Do you think he could've been hurt?" Mom asks with a creased brow.

"If he was hurt, we'd probably know about it, Beth. You'd be hearing your name on the PA system."

"Maybe we should talk to someone," I suggest. "Security or something?"

"We've already paged him," says Steven. "You don't really want to send out a search team for him, do you?"

"I guess not." Mom sighs. "I just wish he'd get down here."

"I wish I'd thought to loan him my phone," I admit.

"I wish we could go home." Steven frowns at the mountain.

It's still light out, but it's only a matter of time before it gets dusky. They've already turned on the big lights, getting ready for night skiing. I am feeling more and more uneasy. Finally I decide it's time to talk to my mom. Privately. She doesn't like hearing about my dreams or visions. They creep her out, and I try to protect her from that. But I'm thinking that when it involves Zach, I have to make an exception.

"Can I talk to you?" I say to Mom in a quiet tone. "Alone?"

She glances at Steven, who seems oblivious to my request, then back at me. "We're going to visit the little girls' room," she tells him. "Will you keep an eye out for Zach? My phone's on."

He nods, still frowning at the slope like he expects to see Zach riding down any minute.

Mom and I go inside, and I begin to explain about last night's dream. I don't go into all the details but only say that my dream involved snow and that Zach really did get hurt.

"Why didn't you tell us this before we came?"

"I don't know," I say, suddenly feeling guilty, like this is my fault. "I guess it's because it just didn't seem like something that could really happen up here. It didn't seem to fit." I think of the fire, the cabin, the gunshot wound—things I didn't tell her.

"But you said that it involved snow and that Zach was hurt. Where else could that happen? It's not as if we have snow in Brighton right now, Samantha. What if your brother is up there on the mountain seriously injured?"

"My dream wasn't like that. It wasn't a snowboarding accident. He had on Adidas tennis shoes, Mom."

"But he was in the snow and hurt?"

I nod, trying to swallow against the lump growing in my throat.

"So, what are you saying, Samantha? What am I supposed to do with this?"

Tears are burning my eyes now. "I don't know. I just thought I should tell you."

"You're the one who works with the cops," she hisses at me. "You're the one who gets these horrible dreams and things. You should have some answers here."

"Just because God gives me these things doesn't necessarily mean they come with answers. It usually takes hard work to figure things out."

"But you think your brother may have been injured?"

"I don't know, Mom. All I can say is that in my dream, it wasn't a snowboarding accident. It was, uh, something else."

"What?" she demands with angry eyes. "Tell me exactly what your dream was. How did Zach get hurt?"

I look down at my snowboarding boots and take in a deep breath as I pray a silent prayer. Should I tell her? Will it help? Or will it hurt?

"I am your mother, Samantha. Tell me."

I look back up at her. "Zach was lying facedown in the snow. There'd been a fire nearby…a cabin was going up in flames. Zach had been shot."

She stares at me with horror in her eyes. "Shot?"

"I didn't want to tell you. I didn't want to think about it. It didn't seem like something that could really happen. Not today. Not here."

"A fire?" she says in a quiet voice. "Why would there be a fire up here in the snow?"

"I know...it doesn't really make sense."

"Was he dead, Sam?" Her face looks pale now. Oh, her cheeks are still flushed from the cold, but beneath that is white, like the blood has drained out.

"I don't know... It didn't look good."

"What do you think it means?"

"I was hoping it was more like a warning dream...more symbolic than a real prediction."

"Symbolic of what?"

"I thought it might be related to drugs, like Zach might be using again, and if that was the case, he was going to get hurt."

Mom puts a hand to her head, as if she's almost faint. "I need to sit down."

We walk over to a bench by the window, and Mom just seems to fold over at the knees as she sits down. I know I've ruined her day—Zach and I both have—and I feel horrible.

I put a hand on her shoulder. "I'm sorry, Mom. Maybe my dream was nothing but a bad dream. Maybe I shouldn't have even told you about it. But I've been worried about Zach off and on all day. I even tried to talk to him...about drugs, you know? But he wouldn't listen. We sort of got into an argument, but then he apologized. And after a while we quit riding together. I couldn't keep up with him. And then he went missing...and I didn't know what to think." I blink back tears now. "I feel like this is my fault."

Mom looks at me. Her eyes are glistening too. "It's not your fault, Samantha. But it's not exactly easy to hear about your dreams, especially when they involve my son."

"It's not exactly easy to have dreams like that." I want

to add that her son is also my brother, but I don't think that'll help much.

Mom stands. "I guess I should go speak to someone, let them know that he's missing and we're worried about his welfare."

I stand too. "Yeah. I think so."

My boots feel like they weigh a ton, like I can barely drag my feet over to the information desk, where my mom talks to a security woman. "My son was supposed to meet us here at three thirty. We only have day passes, and we were trying to leave early. I'm afraid he may have gotten hurt or lost."

The woman looks at Mom with compassion. She asks his name, clothing description, height, weight, and age, writing each thing down on a small pad as Mom tells her.

The woman looks up. "He's *twenty*?"

Mom nods. "Yes, that's right."

The woman frowns. "Well, a twenty-year-old might be off doing just about anything." She looks at the clock. "He's not quite two hours late yet. Have you checked the lounge? We've had some kids sneaking in there with fake IDs about this time of day even though the staff is supposed to stay on top of it."

Mom looks indignant. "I hardly think my son is off drinking in the lounge."

I nudge Mom's elbow as in *hint-hint, he might be.*

"Well, I'll put out an APB on him," says the woman. "Keep your cell phone on, and if I hear anything, I'll give you a call."

"Thank you," my mom says in a crisp voice.

The woman looks at me now. "In the meantime, you might want to look around a bit more."

I know she means we should check the lounge, but I wait until we're out of earshot before I mention it to Mom. "He might be in the lounge. I mean, I know that he and Tate have been drinking buddies lately."

"You know this for a fact?"

I nod, feeling like a traitor. To both my mom and my brother. But really, what should I have done?

"You stay here, Samantha. I'll go check the lounge."

I pray as I wait. And as weird as it seems, I pray that Zach is in the lounge. I mean, seriously, isn't that preferable to being injured—or worse—out in the snow after dark?

Apparently not. I try not to look too happy as Mom emerges from the lounge with Zach in tow. I'm surprised she's not pulling him by his ear. Her face is so angry that I think I might prefer to walk home tonight. And Zach, of course, looks pretty sheepish.

"Do you have any idea what you've put us through?" she is saying to him. "We've been worried sick and—"

"I lost track of time. I thought it was still early and—"

"I don't want any of your excuses, Zach!" She opens her cell and punches the digits of Steven's number with such force that I'm surprised the phone doesn't fall apart in her hand. "You owe all of us, especially Steven, a big fat apology."

"I'm sorry—"

"Shut up!" she snaps. "No, not you, Steven. Sorry. We found Zach." She pauses as he says something. "Yes, he's just fine." She glares at her son. "Well, physically anyway. I have no idea what's wrong with his head." Then they agree to meet at her car.

It's getting dark as we leave the parking lot. No one

speaks, which is a good thing. Steven turns on the radio to a jazz station. He's almost as ticked as my mom, but I'm relieved he doesn't delve into it. I'm also relieved that my brother is okay. At least he's okay for now. Who knows what's around the next corner for him.

We're about twenty minutes from home when my mom finally breaks the silence. "I'm so sorry about how this day ended," she says to Steven. "I had no idea I had raised such a selfish and insensitive son."

"Thanks, Mom." Zach folds his arms across his chest and glares at the back of her head.

Ignoring him, she continues. "I know he's had a drug problem, and I'm afraid that has impaired his thinking even more than I realized. And since he appears to be incapable of taking responsibility for his actions or even making apologies to those he has hurt, I will take it upon myself to—"

"Why don't you just shut up?" shouts Zach.

Okay, now I'm getting scared. This is way over the line. Even for him.

Mom turns around in her seat and stares at him. "What?"

"Everyone just calm down," says Steven. "Zach, that is no way to talk to your mother—"

Then Zach calls Steven a profane name, and I think my mother is about to jump over the seat and kill her son right here on the interstate. I am silently praying now, begging God for help. Any kind of intervention. Mom is so furious she's speechless. Steven seems to have given up.

"Zach," I begin in a controlled but somewhat angry tone. "You are so wrong…about pretty much everything. We've all been fairly patient with you today, considering how you worried us, how you made us wait for you. And for you to act like this, well, it's just totally juvenile."

He turns away from me, looking out the window.

"Well said, Samantha," says Steven.

"Well said," Zach imitates in a hostile tone but quietly enough that I'm the only one to hear.

I just shake my head. Sometimes I can't believe this guy really is my brother. It's like drugs have stolen his soul...addiction is holding his heart ransom. But even as I think this, I know that God is the Great Redeemer. He can deliver Zach from this. If only Zach was willing.

God, help my poor foolish brother. Help Zach to figure this out.

Fifteen

Things do not improve once we get home. Mom and Zach get into one of the worst fights ever. Naturally, this results in Zach walking out. As he's leaving, Mom tells him not to come back. I cringe inwardly and retreat to my room. I hate this. I really hate this.

I hadn't really planned on going out tonight, but I promised Conrad I'd call him when I got home. So I do.

"How was the snow?" he asks cheerfully.

"Okay..."

"Okay? I heard they had six new inches."

"Yeah. I guess it was pretty good."

"You sound bummed, Samantha. Everything okay?"

And that's what unleashes everything. Suddenly I am sobbing. "I'm sorry. I can't really talk about this on the phone."

"Can I come over?"

"It's not very pleasant here." I can still hear Mom thrashing around downstairs. I think she's taking her anger out on the kitchen right now. I expect to hear the sounds of breaking glass at any moment.

"How about if I pick you up? We'll be late, but we can still make it to youth group."

I don't feel like going to youth group tonight. But maybe that's when a person really needs it, so I agree.

"I'll be there in fifteen minutes, okay?"

"Okay," I say meekly. "Thanks."

I attempt to do some quick damage control, but it's useless. Between the wind and sun on the slopes today and my crying jag just now, my face looks red and puffy and pathetic. My uncontrollable curls are safely contained in two braids, which I don't bother to remove. *Here's the test of a good boyfriend,* I think as I pull on a fresh top and study my ravaged image in the mirror. *Can he love this?* I put on some fresh lip gloss and grab my jacket, and just as I'm heading downstairs, the doorbell rings.

"That's Conrad," I call out to Mom. "We're going to youth group."

She mutters something, and I make a quick exit. Conrad immediately hugs me and, with his arm still around my shoulders, leads me to his car and opens the door. I'm surprised at how comforting it feels to be back in his old Gremlin, to feel like he's taking care of me. I lean into the seat and let out a long, tired sigh.

"Want to tell me about it?" he asks as he drives toward the church. So I give him the shortened version of Zach being late, us being worried, him being in the bar, and the mean words and big fight that followed.

"That's too bad." He pulls into the parking lot, but we remain in the car.

"I think it's all because of the addiction," I say sadly. "Despite ninety days of rehab, I don't think Zach is over it yet." Then I confess how I've been extremely worried about my brother. I don't tell Conrad about my dream, but I do tell him that Zach hasn't been working his recovery program. "I actually fear for his safety."

"The drug world's a pretty scary place," he says. "I can't imagine why anyone wants to go there intentionally."

"It's insane."

"Do you want to pray for him?" he offers.

"Yes! Thank you!"

To my weary relief, Conrad does most of the praying, and I do most of the agreeing. And I'm impressed with how well he seems to grasp this whole situation. And how tuned in he is to Zach's problem and how it impacts everyone around him. Finally he asks God to reach down and rescue Zach—from his addiction and from himself. He prays that God will do everything possible to bring Zach to his knees and back to God. Then we both say, "Amen!"

"We're really late now," I point out.

He nods. "I know."

Just then my stomach makes a loud rumbling noise.

He turns and looks at me, then laughs. "Have you had anything to eat tonight?"

"Come to think of it, no."

"Wanna go get a burger or something?"

I grin at him, thinking, *How much better can a boyfriend get?* "Sounds good to me."

I try not to obsess over Zach as Conrad and I put away cheeseburgers, fries, and shakes. I figure the calories aren't going to hurt me much after a high-energy day of snowboarding.

"Feeling better?" he asks as we're walking back to his car.

I nod. "Thanks. You're good medicine."

He leans over and kisses me before he opens the door. "You are too."

"Were you feeling bad about something too?" I ask after he gets into the car. "I was so upset I never even thought to ask."

He kind of shrugs, but the way he does this suggests something is bothering him also.

"What is it?"

"Well, I told you how Katie has been sick the last couple of weeks, and my parents were worried that she didn't seem to be getting better, right?"

"Yes." I immediately remember the first time I met his adorable six-year-old sister—the little redheaded baton twirler. "Didn't your mom take her to the doctor last week?"

"Yeah. But they want to run some more tests."

"More tests?"

"Something in her blood work didn't look right."

I can tell by his voice that this really has him worried. "Do you think it could be a mistake?"

"That's what we're hoping. But the fact is, Katie isn't feeling too well."

"I'm sorry. I hope it's nothing… I hope she's okay."

He nods. "Yeah. Thanks. My parents are trying to act like it's all nothing and everything will be fine. But I can tell they're pretty worried."

"I'll really be praying for her, Conrad."

"Thanks."

"Do you want to pray for her right now?"

He brightens. "Sure. That'd be great."

So this time I take the lead, and Conrad does the agreeing. I really pray for God to intervene here. I ask Him to show the doctors exactly what's wrong with Katie. I ask Him to make her well again. And then I ask Him to give the Stiles family peace in the meantime. "Remind them to put their trust in You," I finally say. "Remind all of us, dear heavenly Father. You love us so much, more than we can even imagine. Remind us that we can take all our cares and our worries straight to You. And You can handle them for us. Amen."

"And amen."

I'm not surprised Zach isn't home when I go into the house later. The truth is, I feel pretty certain he won't be coming home at all tonight. And while this seriously worries me, there's nothing I can do about it besides pray and trust God. I suspect we've just gone back to the old ways where he'll stay out late or disappear for days at a time, and there will be fights. Lots of fights between Zach and Mom.

I am relieved that Mom isn't thrashing around and slamming things anymore. I can see the light under her bedroom door, and I imagine she's reading in bed. I think about knocking on her door and saying something to her, but I hate to disturb her peace. I figure she can hear me. If she wants to talk, she'll come out.

I try to imagine what it would feel like to be her. I know it's not easy, but she makes it a whole lot harder by shutting God out of her life. I don't understand why or how she thinks she can do this alone. Sometimes I wonder if this whole deal with Zach isn't God's way of breaking her, to bring her back to Him. But then I realize that Zach makes his own decisions. And it's really not God's fault that he chooses to do drugs. That's ridiculous. Still,

I believe all things really do work for good when we love God and live for Him. So I'm trying to believe that even Zach's horrible drug problem could be the thing that brings good back into my mom's life. That's what I'm praying for anyway.

I add little Katie to my prayer list. I can't believe how long this list is getting, but then people just keep having problems. Someone's got to be praying. I get ready for bed, read my Bible verses, and then begin to pray. I drift to sleep after only a couple of names, but I know God understands. And He never sleeps.

I check Zach's room in the morning. It's messy, and his bed's not made, but I can tell he hasn't been home, because if he had, he would be asleep right now. But my mom is up. She sits at the breakfast bar, silently sipping coffee as I pour myself a bowl of cereal.

"Going to church?"

"Yes," I tell her. Then as I often do, I invite her to come with me.

She sort of smiles. "Poor Samantha, you live in such a house of sinners."

"Everyone is a sinner, Mom."

She waves her hand. "Oh, I know. But your mom and your brother...well, we're not like you, are we?"

I'm not sure where she's going with this, but I know I'd better watch out. I have a feeling she's still in a bad frame of mind after last night. I just shrug as I take a bite of my Cheerios.

"You're like your dad, Samantha. Just plain good at heart."

"Like I said," I say with cereal still in my mouth, "we're all sinners."

"Yes, yes, I've heard that all before. But some of us just seem to be better at sinning than others."

I try not to roll my eyes as I dig my spoon in again. "Whatever."

"Do you ever wonder what your dad would think if he could see us now?"

I glance over at Mom and get sort of worried. Is she okay? I've never really heard her go on like this before. "Actually," I say slowly, "I like to think Dad can see us. I mean, sometimes. Not always. That would be creepy."

"Seems like it would make him sad to see us…"

"You mean because we're such a mess?"

"Well, not you, Samantha. You seem to have your head on right."

"I make mistakes too, Mom."

"Anyway, I think it would make your dad very sad to see how Zach is doing…and me too. I'm sure he'd be disappointed that I'm not going to church anymore."

I consider this. "You know what I think?"

Her brows arch in interest. "What?"

"I think people in heaven see everything totally differently."

"What do you mean?"

"It's just a feeling, okay, but I think they see things more like how God does. I think they understand that some things, like Zach's problems, are just temporary. Like maybe Dad knows Zach is struggling right now, but he also knows that Zach will eventually beat this and return to God and live a good, productive life."

"You really believe that?"

I nod. "I'm trying to. I guess that's why they call it faith.

I mean, it doesn't look like that's going to happen, but it's what I'm praying for. And I'm sure it's what Dad is praying for. Or, like I said, maybe Dad sees it happening already. He's probably not the least bit worried."

She frowns. "And what do you think your dad sees when he looks at me? That is, if this is even possible, and I'm not really convinced it is. I'm just playing along."

"It's similar to Zach. Dad knows you've had some pretty hard struggles. And of course, he understands why. But I think he can see you beyond those things. I think he knows that you'll give your heart back to God and live a truly happy life again."

She sort of smiles. "You really do have some incredible faith, Samantha."

"Even faith is a gift from God, Mom. We can't really muster it up on our own."

"But you have to be willing, right?"

"Right."

"I guess you should start praying that I'll be willing," she says sadly. "Because the truth of the matter is, I'm not. Not yet anyway. I'm still mad at God. I'm mad at Him for taking your dad...and I'm mad at Him about Zach."

"So you blame Him for those things?"

"Well, everyone says that God controls everything, right?"

I stare at her, trying to understand why she thinks the things she does. Then I carefully answer. "God doesn't control us, Mom. We have our own free will. God didn't control the criminal who shot Dad any more than He controls Zach and the stupid choices he makes. Don't you know that?"

She sighs. "I used to know that. I'm not really sure what I know anymore."

I smile at her. "That's a good reason for you to start coming to church with me again."

"Maybe someday, but not today."

"I'll hold you to that." I pick up my bowl and drink the leftover milk.

"Good. You do that."

I go over to the sink to rinse my bowl, then put it in the dishwasher.

"Samantha?"

"Yeah?"

"I don't know what to do about your brother."

I turn and look at her. "Huh?"

"I think I'm going to have to lay down the law with him."

"What do you mean?"

"I'll have to tell him that he can't live here if he doesn't go to his meetings…continue his recovery…get a job." She looks at me with misty eyes. "Is this unfair?"

I consider this. I mean, it's hard to imagine Zach living on the streets. But on the other hand, he's messing up pretty bad just living at home. "I don't think it's unfair," I finally say.

"I called Zach's rehab place in Washington last night. I actually spoke to Ebony's brother."

"Really?"

"Yes. I needed some advice."

"What did he say?"

"That Zach probably needs tough love."

"Like throwing him out?"

She frowns. "I don't like to think of it that way…but, yes."

"Well, he's probably right, Mom. I'm sure he knows what he's talking about. Ebony says he's really good at this. He's seen a lot. He used to be an addict himself."

"He said I should do it right though. He said not to get angry or turn it into a fight, like I did last night."

"That makes sense."

"He said if I turn it into a fight, Zach can just blame me. And Zach needs to realize that his being kicked out of the house is the result of his own bad decisions. I think that's exactly how Mr. Hamilton put it. He said Zach needs to feel his own consequences and own up to his poor choices."

Okay, now I'm thinking about my dream again. The one with the snow and the burning cabin. And then the one where I was trapped in the burning building. I'm worried that Zach being out on the street could force him into an even more dangerous situation. And yet I do understand what Mom is saying. It's just confusing.

"So do you agree with me on this, Samantha?"

I blink and bring myself back into the conversation. "I think so."

"Because I need you to back me up. Okay?"

"Sure," I promise. "I'll back you."

"I doubt that we'll see Zach before tonight. My guess is he'll show up pretty late, just in time to sneak in and go to bed. But I plan to be waiting for him, and I'll tell him that he can't stay here anymore."

I try to imagine this. I mean, what if it's raining out? What if Zach is sorry? What if he refuses? "So you'll make him leave right then? Even if it's night and he has nowhere to go?"

Mom looks worried now. "Do you think that's too harsh?"

"I don't know…"

"Do I need to rethink this?"

"No, I think you're on the right track, Mom." I consider the whole thing, wishing for a magic answer when there really seems to be none.

"Maybe I should just warn him. I'll tell him the rules have changed. I'll draw a firm line."

"Yes," I say eagerly. "That seems fair. Tell him he has to go to his NA meetings and actually stay for the whole thing, and he must meet with his mentor."

"And he must find a job."

"Yes. Maybe you should actually write those things down. Make it perfectly clear."

"In black and white."

"Yes. No wiggle room."

Mom smiles. "Okay. I think we can do this, but it won't be easy."

I glance at the clock above the stove. "I'd better go, or I'll be late for church. You sure you don't want to come?"

"Not this time."

Okay, that's not exactly a promise. But somehow I feel that my mom has just gotten a couple of inches closer. And as I drive to church, I pray that God will keep working on her, that He will draw her back to Himself, and that she'll be so happy when she gets there, she'll wonder what took her so long.

Sixteen

As I'm driving home from church in my cute little green Bug, it occurs to me that the reason I have this cool ride is so I can help Ebony with police work. Specifically, at least for now, police work aimed at the drug problems in our community.

Okay, this seems incredibly ironic since I'm pretty sure my brother may be toying with some drug dealings of his own. Oh, I don't know this for sure. I mean, so far all I know is that he's been drinking, and I had a bad dream about him that seemed linked to drugs. But I also know that alcohol is often the first step toward other kinds of chemical use. Plus Zach's life isn't exactly on track at the moment. Not a good sign.

So I feel slightly hypocritical. I mean, I'm working with Ebony and the police while my brother is acting like a criminal? How is this supposed to add up? And what if I discover that Zach is involved in something serious? Would I turn him in? Ebony said my job wasn't to get my peers arrested but to try to find out who their connections might be. But what if one of their connections turns out to be my brother? What then?

Once again it seems my only recourse is to pray. I ask

for God to lead me, to help me, and to show me what's right and how to do it. Then I decide to drive around town a bit. Okay, I probably just want to drive, but suddenly I am curious about Tate. Something about this guy never seems to add up. I mean, he supposedly works, but he also has plenty of time to hang with my brother. Maybe I should check up on him. I make a mental note to look into this after school tomorrow.

I drive past where Felicity lives. I still feel haunted by the image of her lying unconscious on that red sofa. What did that mean?

To my surprise, I see a girl who looks a whole lot like Felicity about six blocks from her house. I slow down and take a better look, and when the girl gives me the middle-finger salute, I know it's her.

"Sorry," she says when I stop beside her. "I didn't know it was you. I thought it was some jerk trying to pick me up."

I sort of laugh. "Do you need a ride?"

She frowns, then nods. "Sure."

"Where are you going?" I ask as I continue driving in the direction she was walking. I assume she was going home, but I don't want to admit I know where that is.

"I'm not sure." She opens her purse and takes out a pack of cigarettes. "Mind if I smoke?"

I frown. "Actually…"

She rolls her eyes and throws the pack back into her purse. "Yeah, yeah, I get it. You don't want to stink up your car."

"I guess I'm kind of protective. I haven't had it for very long."

"It's kind of cute, in an obnoxiously perky, happy sort of way." Then she laughs. "You'd never catch me driving something like this."

"Well, it was a good deal," I say sort of apologetically.

"Yeah, whatever." She leans back and lets out a big sigh.

"So where can I take you?"

"Anywhere…" She shakes her head. "I was going home, but I don't even know why. There's nothing there."

I consider this. "Wanna get a coffee?"

She perks up a little. "Sure."

"Lava Java?"

"That's cool."

We drive in silence for a couple of blocks, and suddenly she asks me what I was doing in this neighborhood. "You don't live around here, do you?"

"No, I was actually on my way home from church."

"That sounds about right," she says in a sarcastic tone. "You seem like the type."

"The type?"

"You know, a good girl."

I feel like this is a rerun of the conversation I had with Mom this morning. But I control myself from giving her the exact same sermon. Although I do point out that God loves us all, just the way we are, and that if I'm "good," it must be due to Him.

"Whatever. My mom used to be religious too."

"But not anymore?"

"Now she's just depressed."

"Oh…" I decide to change the subject. "So are you and Jack dating?"

"Dating?" She gets this blank sort of look. "We hang

together… That's about it. It's not like I'm in love with him or anything."

"He seems nice."

"Seriously?"

"Yeah."

"Most people wouldn't agree with you on that."

"I'll admit he can act pretty tough and scary, but I don't think that's who he really is." Then I tell her how I remember him being a nice kid back in middle school.

"Everyone changes."

"Maybe, but parts of us stay the same. We just learn to cover them up. Maybe as a safety device."

"I'm curious, Samantha. That thing you told me the other night, when we crashed the party, was that legit?"

"Of course. Why?"

"It's just weird. I mean, you hardly know me. Why would you get a feeling like that about me? You're not a lesbian, are you?"

I laugh. "No. And if it makes you feel better, I have a boyfriend who I really, really like." Then I tell her a little about Conrad and how he took me for a burger last night and made me feel much better.

"Why were you feeling bad?"

I'm parking near Lava Java now and considering my answer as I carefully pull into the space. Should I tell her the truth? "It's kind of a long story," I say as I turn off the engine.

"Hey, I got nothing but time." She holds up her purse. "The fact is, I'm flat broke. You'll have to buy the coffee."

"No problem."

Once we're inside and seated with our coffees, she persists. "Seriously, Samantha, I want to know why you were feeling bummed last night. It seems like you pretty much have it all going on."

And that's when I decide to tell her about Zach. I figure it's a good way to find out more about her. So, sparing few details, I explain about his meth addiction, his treatment, his recent drinking, and finally how my mom plans to kick him out of the house. "Well, she's going to give him an ultimatum first. He has to abide by her rules, or he's outta there."

"He'll blow it."

"How do you know?"

She smiles, but it's a devilish kind of smile. "I just know."

I frown. "Really? You really think he'll blow it?"

"I think he's *already* blown it."

"What makes you say that?" Okay, I'm getting a little irritated at this girl. I give her a ride, buy her coffee, and she sits here condemning my brother. Just who does she think she is?

"Because I think I know your brother, Samantha. Zach McGregor, right?"

I blink. I thought I was careful not to mention his name. I just kept calling him "my brother." How can she possibly know him?

"Don't look so surprised. Brighton is a small town. I mean, two high schools, one mall—I know a lot of people. Your name is McGregor. You told me enough about your brother. It just adds up."

"Really? You know him?"

"Zach is your brother, isn't he?"

I nod and take a sip of coffee. This is too weird. But then it occurs to me that perhaps God is at work here. "How well do you know him?"

"Well enough to know he's already blown it. He's fallen off the wagon, and I suspect your mom's ultimatum won't mean a thing to him. Oh, he might lie to her, and he might tell her that he'll abide by her stuffy old rules. But just wait. He won't."

"How can you be so sure?"

"It's just what is."

"Oh…"

"Don't get all bummed, Samantha. You seem like a smart girl. You must've known your brother had started using again." She narrows her eyes and peers at me. "And what about your little intuitions? Don't you have them for your own brother?"

"Actually, I did. I guess that's why I was so worried last night."

"Really?" She leans forward with interest. "What kind of feeling did you get for him?"

"A pretty bad one."

"As bad as what you got for me?"

I can't tell if she's teasing me, but I decide to go along. Maybe I'm being a fool, but I'm doing it for God's sake. And for hers. "At least as bad, maybe worse."

"You are just the freakiest girl, Samantha." She laughs so loudly that other coffee patrons turn and look. "*Samantha!* I just remembered—that's the name of one of my favorite sitcom characters. Have you ever heard of *Bewitched*?"

"Yes." I try not to groan at this connection. "It's not like I live under a rock, you know."

"Maybe you're like *that* Samantha. Maybe you're a witch like her and that's why you have these special powers to know what's going to happen to someone, and you—"

"I am not a witch," I say in a stiff voice. "I'm a Christian. And any special power I have is a gift from God. And it's to help people."

"Really?" She doesn't look convinced, and I am getting irritated.

"And you're making me sorry that I even told you about it."

"I'm sorry…" She actually seems somewhat sincere now.

"Well, I have feelings too."

"Yeah, I know. I can be pretty mean sometimes. My shrink said it's because I've been hurt so much that I lash out to hurt others."

"You have a shrink?"

"Not anymore. The state paid for a few sessions last year. Then the funding ran out, and I had to come up with new ways to deal with my anger."

"Like what?"

"Like whatever it takes."

"I suspect you do drugs," I say slowly. "But I hope you're not like my brother. I hope you don't do meth."

She looks down at her coffee.

"Do you?"

"What?"

"You know, do you do meth?"

"I've tried it."

"Tried it?"

"Yeah, meaning I don't do it all the time. Sheesh, who can afford that?"

"So you're not an addict?"

"Look at me." She actually pulls up her sleeves and shows me her arms. "Do I look like an addict? Do I have scars? Do I have lesions? Crud, I'm not even under-weight, which is one of the perks that's actually appealing."

I make a face. "Seriously? You think that's appealing?"

"You don't know me, Samantha. You don't know how my mind works. It's not like yours, okay? I can't go to church to feel good. I'm not a *good* girl. Don't you get that?"

"I know we're different. But for some reason, I care about you. And, no, I'm not a lesbian. I just think God has put you on my heart for a reason."

"So you honestly believe that God is responsible for that feeling you had about me—about being in danger?"

"I do."

"Was it a threat from God? Is He going to punish me for something?" She swears now. "Like I haven't been punished enough."

"No, I don't believe God is going to punish you," I say quickly. "I believe the reason He showed me that…that vision was because He loves you and wants to protect you from getting seriously hurt."

She pushes a strand of bright blue hair away from her eyes. "It's just hard to swallow. I mean, why should I believe you? And even if I did believe you, what would I do differently? How could I prevent whatever it is you think is going to happen from happening? How would I even know?"

"For one thing, you could stay away from drugs."

She just laughs.

"No, I mean it. You know drugs aren't good for you. You know people get hurt by them all the time. They ruin lives."

Her eyes have a blank look now, and I can tell she's blocking me out.

"I know you've heard that before, and nothing I tell you is going to make any difference, right? Like talk to the hand?"

She nods. "Yeah."

"What if I tell you about the specific impression I got for you? Would that help?"

"You have specifics?"

I nod.

"Sure. Go for it."

Now, even though I like to keep my "gift" a secret, I am learning that sometimes, in some cases, I need to tell about it in order to get through to a person. I think this is one of those times. "Okay...," I begin slowly. "I sometimes get these little flashes of insight, kind of like a vision, where I see something really quick, and then it's gone. It's usually a warning." I look closely at her, trying to gauge whether or not she's taking me seriously. Convinced that I really do have her full attention, I continue. But first I force myself to remember that vision. "About a week ago I got this flash image of you. Your face was very pale, and you seemed to be unconscious. You had one hand draped over your mouth, and the other hand seemed twisted behind your back. I noticed a hypodermic syringe nearby, and you were lying on a beat-up, old red sofa."

"A red sofa?"

I nod. "Do you have a red sofa?"

"Nope."

"But you know someone who does?"

She nods, and with a look of realization, her eyes get wider, like maybe she actually believes me now. Then suddenly she starts laughing like this is a joke. "Man, you had me going there for a minute, Samantha."

"What do you—?"

"That whole red sofa bit. Nice try."

"Huh?"

"Obviously, you've seen it, haven't you?"

"I saw it in my vision."

"Yeah, right. Your vision." She rolls her eyes. "No, I mean, you've seen that old, beat-up red sofa for real, right?"

Okay, now I'm confused. "What do you mean?"

"At Tate's apartment."

"Tate's apartment? As in Tate Mitchell?"

"As in Tate, your brother's friend. I'm sure you've been to his place before, right? You saw the sofa, and you—"

"No, I've never been to Tate's apartment. I don't even know where he lives. Actually I thought he lived with his parents."

"His parents?" She laughs. "Yeah, right."

I'm trying to take this in. "Tate has a beat-up red sofa?"

"He most certainly does."

"Where does he live?"

"You really don't know?"

"Honestly, I don't."

She presses her lips together and looks at me with suspicion in her eyes. "Why don't you ask your brother?"

I'm worried now, like I've probably taken this too far. I can't blow my cover. "Yeah, maybe I will."

"In the meantime, you might need to work on your act, Samantha. You know, before you take it on the road or anything." She laughs again.

Now I'm trying not to get mad at her meanspirited ignorance, trying not to feel defensive. But she seems to be insulting God as much as me.

"It's not an act," I say in a quiet but serious tone. "I think God is trying to warn you about something very significant. But it's your choice whether you listen or not. And since I've told you my vision, the next step is up to you."

I look straight into her eyes now. "But I will be very sad if I see your photo on the six o'clock news some night and if I hear the newscaster saying you died of a drug overdose. And I will be especially sad if I find out it happened on an old red sofa. You can take it or leave it."

Seventeen

On Monday after school I go straight to the police station—although I park my conspicuous car over by the park district building where Mom works. It makes a nice cover for a bright green car. It turns out that Ebony is working on another case, a domestic situation that erupted into a murder-suicide during the weekend.

"She probably won't be back in for a while," one of Ebony's associates tells me. "You can call her on her cell if you like."

"I just needed to do some research. I need to look up an address for someone that—"

"Check with Bernice," he says as he reaches for his ringing phone. "She's a computer whiz."

I thank him and go off to hunt down Bernice Waters, an older woman who has been on the force for a long time.

"Hi there, Samantha," she says when I find her at work on her computer. "What's up?"

I tell her I'm working on something and need an address.

"For the drug task force?"

I nod. "I've gotten some leads."

"Good for you." Then she shows me how to access the file system and how to find an address. It's amazing how simple it is. I make some notes, then thank her for the help.

"There's a spare computer over there." She points to a desk in the corner. "Make yourself at home."

So I do, and after just a couple of minutes I find Tate's addresses—one for his parents on Lambert Lane and another one for apartment 214 on Grant Avenue. My best guess is that the address on Grant Avenue belongs to the run-down apartment building across from the movie-theater complex, the place where I thought I saw Tate and Zach not that long ago. My only questions now are, does this apartment have an old red sofa, and how can I get inside to find out?

I decide to swing by the automotive store that Tate's uncle supposedly owns and where Tate supposedly works. I'm halfway tempted to park and go inside and ask around, but that could backfire on me. Then to my surprise, I see Tate's dark blue Toyota coming around from the back of the store. My brother is sitting in the passenger seat looking at Tate, which means he doesn't see me. But I keep my eyes straight ahead and continue to drive on past. It's a busy street, and there's no reason I shouldn't be driving down it. For all anyone would know, I could be on my way to the mall. Even so, my heart is pounding with fear. And now I don't particularly want to be seen driving past the apartment complex where Tate lives.

I finally decide to go by the mall. Just in case. But I simply park my car, and then I call Olivia.

"Are you done meeting with Ebony?" she asks.

"It wasn't really a meeting."

"Everything okay? You've been so quiet lately, Sam. It's like you've been someplace else."

"I guess I have a lot on my mind." I really wish I could tell her about my participation on the task force—and my fear that my own brother may be involved in something dangerous…something criminal. I need to talk to someone.

"Why don't you come over to Lava Java?" she suggests. "I'm here with Alex and Garrett."

"It's tempting," I tell her. And it really is. "But I have some things I need to do. Thanks anyway."

We hang up, and I just sit here for a while. I don't even know why I'm here or what I'm doing, but I need to do something. Finally I pray. I ask God to lead me. And then, feeling calmer, I drive over to Grant Avenue. My plan is simply to drive past the apartment complex. If I see Tate's car again, I will just act normal and keep driving. But I'm hoping I can figure out which apartment is his. Oh, I don't plan to knock on the door or attempt to break in or anything stupid. I just want to know for future use.

To my relief, I don't see his car anywhere. So I drive through the trashy-looking parking lot and look at the numbers of the apartments until I finally figure out that number 214 is probably located directly above 114. It's on a corner, and I'm guessing one of the windows looks out onto Grant Avenue and toward the theater complex.

I drive back around and spot the apartment from the street. The blinds on the window facing the street appear to be closed. Even so, I don't allow myself to stare up at it. I just drive past and head toward home. Okay, I don't know how anything I've done this afternoon helps anyone. But maybe it's groundwork of some kind.

As I pull into our driveway, my phone begins to ring, and it's Ebony. She heard I was at the station and wants to know if everything's okay.

"I think I might be onto something," I tell her. "A girl at my school, the one I had that vision about, has been talking to me. I'm trying to follow something up."

"Do you need help?"

"Not yet."

"You're being safe? Keeping a distance?"

"Absolutely."

"Good."

"I'm just trying to piece some things together."

"Any names you want to run by me?" She sounds hopeful.

"Not yet." Okay, now I have that shaky feeling inside the pit of my stomach again. I mean, what am I doing here? For Pete's sake, I'm talking about my very own brother and his friend. How can I participate in something that could get these guys into serious trouble? *How can I not?*

I'm tempted to tell Ebony about my last vision, the one with Zach facedown in the snow. But I'm not sure it will help anything, because I'm really beginning to think it was a metaphor. Like my mom said, playing with drugs is like playing with fire. You will get burned. And even the whole snow thing is sort of like drugs—you stay in it too long and you die of exposure. Okay, that doesn't explain the gunshot wound.

"So you'll stay in touch then?" asks Ebony.

"Yeah, of course."

I'm just getting out of my car when Mom pulls into the driveway with a worried look on her face. I wave and go inside. She's stressing over Zach. He hasn't come home since the big fight. I think it's probably a good thing. And now that I've seen him, I can at least tell her he's alive and well. Okay, I don't know if he's well or not, but he was breathing. She comes in, and I relay my information in a quick, casual way.

"Where were they?" she asks as she sets her purse down.

"The automotive store where Tate works."

"Was he working?"

"I don't know, Mom. I just happened to be driving by."

She frowns. "Maybe Zach is getting a job there too."

"Yeah, maybe..." Of course, I doubt this.

"Well, at least he's okay."

"Right."

"How's Katie?" I ask Conrad during lunch on Wednesday. I know she had tests on Monday. "Any results back yet?"

He shakes his head. "Not yet."

"I've really been praying for her," says Olivia.

"Me too," adds Alex.

"I'd pray too," says Garrett, "if I thought it'd do any good."

"Of course it would do some good," says Conrad.

"Yeah," says Alex. "Haven't you heard about those scientific studies where people prayed for sick people and they got better?"

Garrett frowns. "Scientific?"

"Well, that's what they said. They had two test groups. One that got prayer and one that—"

"Anyway," I interrupt. "Prayer definitely works."

"Did I tell you guys that I asked Maxwell Price to audition for Stewed Oysters?" Olivia says suddenly.

"No way," says Conrad. "Maxwell Price in the Oysters?"

"That is pretty bizarre," I admit. "Is he going to do it?"

"Well, we had a long talk last night," she says. "I explained that I didn't want him to come in there like it was his personal little evangelism project and turn everyone off with his sermons and lectures."

"And?" Alex impatiently nudges her to continue.

"He said he wants to give it a shot."

"But do the Oysters want to give him a shot?" asks Conrad.

"They're desperate for a bass player," Olivia says. "We have another gig—a middle-school dance on Friday, so it should be safe."

"Man, would I love to see old Maxwell up there with the Stewed Oysters," says Alex, "but my family is taking off for spring break that afternoon."

"Where to?" I ask.

"My mom is dragging us all up to Victoria, BC."

"I've heard it's beautiful up there," I say.

"Girls like it." Alex makes a face. "My sisters are thrilled."

We all laugh. Then the others tell about their plans for spring break. I already know that Olivia leaves for an Alaskan cruise on Saturday. And Garrett told me that his foster parents want to take him to meet one of their kids over in Idaho. But it's a surprise to me that Conrad's family has suddenly decided to make a break for Disneyland.

"My dad just got tickets online last night," he tells us. "It was actually a pretty good deal, I guess because it was last minute."

"It'll be packed down there," warns Alex. "Get ready to stand in some megalong lines, bro."

Conrad nods. "We know. But it's what Katie wants to do."

"Well, I hope you guys have a great time," I say.

"How about you, Sam?" asks Garrett.

I shrug. "Well, my mom works…so I guess I'll just hang out."

"Poor Sam," says Olivia. "I wish you could come with us."

I force a smile. "Hey, you could end up with some weird cruise disease or hit an iceberg or something."

"Yeah," says Conrad, "and we'll probably get sunburned and have a heatstroke down in sunny California."

"And I'll die of boredom from looking at flowers and dishes and lace and girlie junk," adds Alex.

"Or maybe you'll develop your feminine side," teases Garrett.

"You're probably the lucky one," Olivia says to me. "You get to do whatever you want for a whole week. You can sleep in, read good books, and just plain relax."

I know they're all acting like I've got the best deal just to make me feel better. But I play along, attempting to suppress my vacation envy. And as I go to class, I remind myself that my heavenly Father owns the whole world and there's no place better to be than right where He wants me to be—even if it is only Brighton. But still, I'm only human, and the idea of being pampered on a cruise ship does sound tempting.

By Friday, I'm actually looking forward to spring break. Some downtime sounds pretty good to me. Felicity wasn't at school again today, and I suspect she's skipping. As I'm going to my car, I notice Jack in the parking lot.

He's alone, just leaning against his pickup. But he looks bummed, so I go over to ask if everything is okay. Am I snooping or just concerned? Sometimes the lines get blurry, but I don't think it can hurt.

"Hey, Jack," I say as I approach him.

"What's up?" A shadow of suspicion crosses his brow as I get closer.

"Nothing." I pause and switch the strap of my bag to my other shoulder. "Just saying hey. I missed Felicity in journalism today. Everything okay with her?"

He shrugs. "I guess…"

"I figured she was probably just skipping."

"Or lying around dead on a red couch?" He peers curiously at me.

"She told you?"

"Uh-huh."

"I didn't tell her about that to scare her," I say. "I was just trying—"

"I know…" He lets out an exasperated sigh. "She said you meant well, but she just happens to think you're a little insane."

I force a smile. "She's probably not the only one."

He frowns now. "So Zach McGregor is your brother?"

"Yep." I control myself from adding, "and he makes me so proud."

He scratches his head. "Just doesn't compute."

"I know," I say in a joking tone. "We don't look much alike, do we?"

"I didn't mean that."

"So you know Zach?"

"Not real well. Felicity introduced me to him at a party."

It figures. "Did you meet his buddy Tate?"

Jack nods. "Yeah, it was his party."

"Oh…" Now an idea hits me. "And did Tate have a red sofa?"

Jack laughs. "Man, what is it with you and red furniture?"

"Well, I just wanted to make sure that Felicity wasn't pulling my leg."

"So you really haven't been to Tate's? You didn't see it?"

I hold out my hands as if to show him who I am. "Do I look like I hang with guys like Tate?"

"What about your brother?"

"Look," I say in a serious voice. "Don't get me wrong. I totally love my brother. But I'm pretty sure he's messing up. And that makes me really mad. He did a ninety-day treatment program for meth, and it seems like he needs to go straight back to it."

Jack kind of nods like he agrees.

"Why do you hang with these guys, Jack? I thought you weren't into the hard stuff."

"I'm not."

I give him a look that's meant to convey skepticism. "Uh-huh?"

"I'm really not. I drink some. And I smoke weed now and then. But I don't do meth. That's a line I won't cross."

"Why?"

He shrugs.

"I'm just curious, Jack. I mean, I can't figure out my brother. Anything you can tell me might help me understand Zach."

"My dad was a heroin addict."

"Oh…" I consider this. "But you say 'was.' Is he over it now?"

"In a way." Jack pulls out a pack of cigarettes. "He's dead."

"Wow...I'm sorry, Jack."

He just nods, then shakes out a cigarette.

I watch as he lights up a Camel. "My dad was murdered," I say quietly. Okay, I'm not even sure why. It just came out.

"I know."

"You know?"

"Man, everybody knows, Sam. It was all over the place back when it happened. We all felt bad for you."

I don't know why this surprises me, but it does. "I guess I was kind of checked out at the time. Not really paying attention, you know?"

"I know."

"When did your dad die, Jack?"

"When I was pretty little. Not even in school yet. The truth is, I barely remember it. He was gone so much anyway. I remember the funeral, but that's about it."

"Still, it's gotta hurt."

He takes a long drag and slowly lets it out. "Yeah. And it hurts even more when your mom keeps comparing you to him."

"But you really don't want to be like him, right? I mean, when it comes to doing hard drugs."

"Yeah. I gotta draw the line."

"But do you worry that dabbling in things like weed or alcohol might make you cross that line?"

"The old gateway drugs thing?"

"Whatever."

"The thought crosses my mind sometimes."

"And yet you don't stop?"

He studies his half-smoked cigarette. "Not yet."

"But you're concerned about Felicity?"

He frowns at me, and I'm afraid I pushed too hard.

"Well, I worry about her," I admit. "I don't want to hear about her dying on anyone's old sofa, red or whatever."

"Me neither."

"Do you miss your music, Jack?"

He shrugs, but I can tell by his eyes that I hit a sore spot.

"Did you hear they got a new bass player?"

He looks curious now.

I sort of laugh. "I don't know how long it'll last," I admit. Then I tell him a little about Maxwell, and he actually laughs too.

"Serves them right."

"Why were you so down on Olivia?" I ask. "You acted so hateful to her, Jack, like you wanted to kill her. And yet you don't really seem like that kind of guy. I mean, you put on a good act, and you even had me scared."

"I don't *hate* Olivia," he says slowly. "I just really dislike these rich kids, you know? The ones with their fancy houses, fancy cars, important parents…acting like they own the school, own the world and the universe. It just makes me wanna puke or punch someone."

I nod. "I can understand that."

"I guess Olivia's okay…"

"Seriously?"

"Yeah. And she can sing too."

"So why did you get kicked out of the band, Jack? I sort of assumed it was because you were into some hard drugs…since Cameron and the others drink and stuff."

"Cameron's mom caught me smoking weed at their house and threw a fit. That was the end of that. In some ways, I was glad."

"But are you still glad?"

He snuffs his cigarette out beneath his heel, then shrugs. "I dunno."

"Am I bugging you with all these questions?"

"Sort of…but not really."

"I guess I'm just curious."

"It's okay."

"Then can I ask you one more nosy question? And you don't have to answer."

He frowns now, and I think I may have gone too far, but then he says, "Okay."

"Well, remember Amanda's birthday party, the one that got busted?"

He laughs. "Yeah. I got out of there just in time."

"Had you been in Olivia's car that night?"

He shrugs.

"Did you leave that Ziploc baggie there?"

His face turns stony. But I think I have my answer.

"Look, it's not like I'm trying to get you arrested," I assure him. "I've just been wondering. It seemed to add up."

He still doesn't say anything.

"I mean, I was pretty mad that night. It wasn't cool getting arrested and being hauled down to city hall."

He snickers. "I heard about that. But I also heard you girls got off."

"After we were humiliated and had to take a drug test."

"Welcome to my world."

I scowl at him now. "That's your choice, Jack. It wasn't ours. We got dragged into it. Do you think that's fair?"

"Hey, I wasn't thinking too clearly that night. And I was mad they'd let a girl into the band. I'm sorry you got into trouble, okay?"

"Okay."

"You should think about being a cop, Sam. You seem like you have a natural instinct for it."

I laugh to cover my surprise at this. "Thanks, but no thanks. Remember that's how my dad got killed."

He nods. "Yeah..."

Just then a couple of his buddies head this way, and I think it's a convenient time to exit. "Take care, Jack. If you see Felicity, give her my best."

He laughs like he knows how she'll react. "Sure, you bet."

"See ya." I head back over to my car feeling rather pleased with myself. Okay, it's not like I really uncovered anything in that little interrogation that I didn't already know, but it seemed like something good happened just now. I'm not sure what exactly, but I'll be praying for Jack more than ever. And for Felicity too. But she seems like a much tougher case to me. Funny how that is. I never would've guessed it to be like that a few weeks ago when I had Jack pegged as the "tough guy" and Felicity as the "victim." Go figure.

I think about my brother as I drive toward home. Zach hasn't shown his face at our house in days. At least not while we were home. Mom thinks he's been by to pick up some of his things, and she's okay with that. I think she hopes he'll stay away until he decides to toe the line, if that ever happens. But I'm starting to feel irritated with him. And scared. I hate to think of where he's going to end up. I wish there was something I could do to get to him.

I decide to drive past Tate's apartment, because I'm curious as to whether Zach is actually staying there or not. Although I can't imagine where else he might be. I just wish I could "happen" to run into him. I'm not even sure what I'd say, but I'd like to talk to him. Okay, I'd like to shake him and yell at him and tell him to straighten up before it's too late. But I'd also like to encourage him. I'd like him to know that I don't want to give up on him—ever. And I'd like to tell him I believe in him. I believe that with God, he can beat this thing. Even so I'm worried. Really worried.

As much as I try to shove it away, that image of Zach lying facedown in the bloody snow still haunts me. But I don't see any sign of Zach or Tate as I drive down Grant Avenue. Knowing I might be pressing my luck, I decide to drive past the automotive store as well. I really don't expect to see them and almost hope that I don't since I don't want them to see me. But once again I notice Tate's car coming around from the back of the building. And once again Zach is riding with him. I glance at my watch to see that it's a little before four. It's possible they've both put in a day of work and are going home now. Or maybe that's just wishful thinking.

I don't look their way but keep my eyes on the street in front of me and just continue driving like this is completely normal. But once again, my heart is pounding hard, and I feel afraid. Why?

I rationalize with myself as I drive home. Why should I be afraid? Zach is my brother. No way would he hurt me. No way would he let anyone else hurt me. I believe that to my core. And yet I still feel scared, like I'm in over my head. And then I realize it's time to pray.

I feel a little better by the time I get home. I park my car in the driveway and lock it as usual, double-checking to make sure it's really secure. Is paranoia kicking in? Then I go into the house and lock and deadbolt the front door behind me, double-checking it too, and even secure the chain-link lock that Mom installed a few years ago for extra safety. At the time, Zach and I teased her, pointing out that anyone could break through those flimsy things. But she told us it was a way to check who was at the door without being totally vulnerable. I lock the back door too, like I'm trying to turn our house into a fortress. Like, who do I think is after me? I try not to obsess over my behavior as I get a soda and what's left of a bag of tortilla chips and take them to my room, where I close my door, wishing I had a lock for it too. Is that weird or what?

I put on a CD, an inspirational group that usually lifts my spirits, and proceed to eat my snack and block out whatever is making me feel so uneasy. I actually consider calling Ebony, but I have no idea what I'd say. That I had a long conversation with a guy whose dad died of a heroin overdose, then saw my brother and his friend in a car, and now I'm spooked? What sense does that make? So again I pray. I ask God to protect me and take these feelings of fear away. I remind myself that God's perfect love gets rid of fear.

Just as I'm starting to relax, I hear someone banging on the door downstairs. My heart begins to pound again, and I think maybe my fears were legit. I grab my cell phone, ready to call 911 as I creep down the stairs.

"Samantha?" yells my brother through the cracked-open front door. He obviously had his key but couldn't get past the chain without doing some damage. "Open up, okay? It's just me, Zach."

Feeling relieved, I hurry down and undo the chain and open the door. But when I see Tate standing next to him, I feel uneasy again.

"What's up?" I ask, pretending to be cool with this.

"Why are you turning this place into Fort Knox?" asks Zach as he and Tate press through the door and past me.

"There've been some break-ins," I say quickly. "Not far from here."

"Oh, well, you can't be too safe." Zach laughs.

"What're you doing here?" I ask.

"Picking up my snowboarding stuff."

"Your snowboarding stuff?"

"Yeah. We're going up to the mountain," says Tate. "Zach was bragging about how great he was last week, and I decided to take him on."

Zach laughs. "Yeah, and we got a sweet deal. Tate's uncle is letting us use his place for the weekend."

"Two full days of riding," says Tate. "Great way to start spring break."

Like these party boys need a break. Do they ever even work? But I just smile and act like that's cool, following Zach up the stairs. Fortunately, Tate remains downstairs. "Need any help?" I ask as Zach goes into his room.

"Huh?"

I go into his room and close the door behind me. "Why are you doing this, Zach?" I begin.

"Doing what?" He turns and stares at me.

"You know what."

He just shakes his head. "I'm just living my life, Sam. Mom doesn't want me here, and I'm doing the best I can on my own."

"I know you're doing drugs, Zach."

He narrows his eyes. "You don't *know* anything."

"I do too," I insist. "I have friends who know you and Tate. You both do drugs. Serious drugs."

He laughs. "Well, you've been misinformed by your so-called friends. Who are they anyway?"

"Like I'm going to tell you."

"Why don't you just bug off, Sam?"

I stand there fuming at my brother as he digs through his messy closet for his snowboarding gear. I haven't handled this right. "Sorry," I say quickly. "I'm just so worried about you, Zach. And Mom said it's okay for you to come back here to live. You just have to stay clean and go to meetings and work. That's not too much to ask, is it?"

He mumbles something I can't hear, but I don't think I want to hear it either.

"I don't want you to get hurt, Zach," I plead with him. "I love you, and I know you're playing with fire. I know you're—"

"Just stay out of it, Sam!" He turns to face me with his snowboard boots in one hand, a jacket in the other. "This is my life. I'm doing the best I can. Maybe it's not the way you'd do it, but then I'm not you. I'm not perfect."

"Nobody's perfect, Zach. I just want you to stay alive. I want you to get well."

He holds out his arms. "Look at me. I'm alive. I'm well. I'm going to have a great weekend. Be happy for me." He tosses me his boots. "Can you carry those for me?"

I pick up his boots and sigh. "Zach, you are going down a dead-end street. Can't you see that?"

He finds an old duffel bag and shoves his gloves and stuff into it. "All I can see is that my little sister is a worry-wart. You're going to have gray hair before you turn twenty, Sam." He tosses me his charmer's smile.

"You may not live to be twenty-one," I tell him in a somber voice.

"See," he says, "there you go again, Ms. Dismal. You really need to lighten up, little sister."

"You really need God, Zachary. You need to surrender your life to Him and let Him help you outta this mess. You can't do it without Him. You need to—"

"I need to get outta this house," he says as he pushes past me and opens the door, then clatters down the stairs, yelling to Tate. "Ready to go, man? We're burning daylight!"

I stay on his heels, lugging his boots along with me, following them out to the driveway, where it's beginning to drizzle. "Zach, I just—"

"Is that your car, Samantha?" asks Tate, nodding toward my Bug as Zach takes his boots from me and throws them into Tate's trunk.

"Yeah."

Tate frowns at me. "I've been seeing this car around town a lot lately. Have you been stalking me or something?"

I suppress my shock and quickly say, "Yeah, right!" Then I force a laugh. "The same thing happened to me right after I got this car." I look directly into his eyes now. "I kept seeing lime green Volkswagens everywhere I went. Finally my friend Olivia told me that happens to everyone after they get a new car. Anyway, I guess there are quite a few of them around here. Who knew?"

"So you haven't been stalking me then?"

I laugh again. "Why would I do that?"

"We gotta go," says Zach, tossing me a warning glance.

I look at my watch for a distraction. "You think you'll make it up there in time for a night pass?"

"They're not open at night," says Tate in an irritated tone.

"Oh, you're not going to Hood?"

Zach frowns at me. "We're going somewhere else. Like it's any of your business." Then he gets into the car and slams the door like a personal message to me. And as they're driving away, it occurs to me that Zach is wearing the same denim jacket he had on in my dream. I feel sick.

I run into the house and grab my cell phone and, with shaking hands, hit my speed dial for Ebony's number. I wait as it rings again and again—*Ebony, please pick up!*—but finally it goes to her message service.

"Please call me, Ebony," I beg. "Something is up. I need your help." Then I hang up and pray she'll call right back. I decide to try her office as well, but again I get her machine. I leave a similar message. And then, with my phone in my pocket, I start pacing. I'm tempted to get in my car and head up to…where? Where would I go? Not Mount Hood. They never did say exactly where they were going. I run up to my room and turn on my computer to see which ski resorts do *not* have night skiing. It takes awhile, but I finally narrow it down. I eliminate the ones on the other side of the state. I can't imagine those party boys wanting to drive seven hours on a Friday night. This leaves one possibility that's only a couple of hours away.

It's five thirty now, but I suddenly remember that Zach mentioned they're staying at Tate's uncle's place. I wonder if the uncle's store is still open or if I can find out his name. I go to the yellow pages and look up the automotive store. Unfortunately, it's only called Chuck's Auto Parts. Not terribly helpful. But I punch in the numbers and pretend to be a customer, disguising my voice as a little old lady's, or so I hope. "I was in your shop just a few days ago looking for an alternator for a 1966 Chevy," I say to the woman who answers. Okay, I have no idea what an alternator is, but Mom had to replace hers a couple of months ago. "And the nice young man, I believe it was the owner of the store, I can't recall his name, Mr.…" I pause.

"Chuck Denton?"

"Yes, that sounds right, dear. Well, as it turns out, my son-in-law found an alternator for me, so you can cancel my order. The name is Eleanor Smith, dear. Thank you very much." Then, with a pounding heart, I hang up. I write *Chuck Denton* and the name of the ski resort on a slip of paper and put it in my pocket. Like I'm going to get amnesia and forget. Then I check my phone to make sure Ebony didn't try to call while I was on the phone. No such luck.

I decide to go and check the landline phone. Not that Ebony would try to reach me at that number, but I'm antsy, and it's a way to pass time. To my surprise, the little red light is flashing. Since it wasn't flashing earlier, maybe someone called when I was outside with Zach and Tate. I play the message and find that it's Mom. She won't be home tonight because she and Steven are going into Portland for a concert that he unexpectedly got tickets to. "It'll probably go until midnight," she says happily, "so don't wait up." I almost consider calling her to tell her that Zach's been here, that he and Tate are going snowboarding, and that Zach is wearing the same denim jacket as in my dream. I can't remember if he had on his Adidas or not. But then I realize I could be alarming my mom for no good reason. I could be alarming everyone for no good reason. Just then my cell phone rings. It's Ebony.

"What's going on?" she asks.

"It's a long story," I quickly say, "and it involves Zach."

"Oh…" I hear the disappointment in her voice, like she suspects which way this is going. "Just start at the beginning, Samantha, and tell it to me slowly."

First I tell her that Zach has not been doing his recovery program and that Mom and I suspect he's gotten back into drugs.

"It's not surprising," she says sadly. "But that doesn't make it any easier. I'm sorry to hear it."

Then I tell her about the dream I had last week and how we went snowboarding the next day and Zach went missing and I assumed the worst. "But it turned out he was just in the bar with a fake ID."

"Uh-huh."

"So then I thought maybe the dream was supposed to be a metaphor for drugs...how they're dangerous. I mean, it's not like we have snow in Brighton."

"Not usually. And certainly not in late March."

"Right." Then I tell her about Tate and Zach going snowboarding for the weekend. "They're on their way up there right now."

"Do you know which resort?"

I explain what they said about the place not having night skiing and my research. She seems to agree. "And, oh yeah," I say suddenly, "they're staying at Tate's uncle's place. I don't know where it is, but I found out his name by calling the automotive store that he owns."

"Chuck Denton?"

"That's right. Do you know him?"

"I know of him."

"As in?"

"As in he's on one of my lists."

"Oh..." Then I tell her about how Tate supposedly works there but is hardly ever there. "Although I've seen him leaving a couple of times. With Zach."

"Uh-huh." I can hear tapping sounds, and I suspect she's doing something on her computer right now.

"So…do you think Zach is in danger?"

"What do you think?"

I consider this now, unsure whether I want to admit what I think. Finally I say, "Yes. I think he's in very serious danger." Then I fill Ebony in on what I've learned from Felicity. How she's confirmed that both Zach and Tate are into drugs in a fairly big way. "In fact, I'm worried about her too. She wasn't in school again today. Her boyfriend hadn't heard from her either."

"You think the vision of the overdose is the real thing, Samantha?"

"I don't know… I mean, it seems a real possibility. But the last time I felt certain she was in danger, poof, she showed up and was just fine. Then when I warned her and told her specifically why I was worried, she just blew me off."

"And that surprised you?"

"No, I guess not." Then I remember something. "She did mention that Tate has an old red sofa in his apartment."

"And did she mention doing drugs there?"

"Not specifically, but that was the insinuation."

"Hmmm…"

"What do we do?"

"For starters I'll do some quick research and see if I can track down Chuck Denton's place up in the mountains. Then I'll have to hand this over to the local authorities up there since it's out of my jurisdiction."

"What will you tell them?"

"Well, based on all you've told me as well as the

dream you described, I suspect that Zach and Tate are involved in some trafficking."

"You think they're delivering drugs?"

"Or picking them up…and something is probably going to go wrong. When a transaction like that results in violence, it's usually because one or both parties tries to double-cross the other. Greed can get ugly."

"Right…" I feel a lump growing in my throat. Like maybe this really is going to be the end of Zach. *Dear God, protect him.*

"Can you give me a detailed description of the cabin you saw burning in your dream, Samantha? Like, how big do you think it was? How were the windows and doors arranged? Any distinctions that might help the police to identify it."

So I get out my notebook where I originally wrote down the dream and relay it all back to her.

"I'm so glad you record these things. Our memory skills aren't completely reliable. But if you write things down, you can count on it."

"And then, of course, there was the fire," I say lamely. "If they see smoke coming from a wooded location…"

"It'll be too late?"

"I suppose…"

"Let me check into some of these things and get back to you, okay? Do you plan on being around this evening?"

"Yes. I'm not going anywhere." I guess it was a good thing I declined Olivia's invitation to watch her and the Oysters at the middle-school dance tonight. My excuse was that I was too old. But suddenly I feel very young, very afraid, and very vulnerable. If Olivia weren't busy,

I'd probably call her up and ask her to come over and hold my hand. I consider calling Conrad, but they're getting ready to fly out early in the morning. And there's the thing with Katie. I can't bug him. No, this is just between God and me right now. And so I really begin to pray. I beg God to protect Zach, to send angels or law enforcers or anything. Just don't let him get hurt.

It's close to seven when Ebony calls back. "I've got a search warrant for Tate's apartment," she tells me. "Eric and I are going to go check it out. Do you want to come along? I was thinking you might pick up on something we would miss."

"Maybe get a vibe from that ugly red sofa?" I say in a semiteasing tone.

She sort of laughs. "We'll take any help we can get."

"The good thing is that you don't have to worry about them being there," I say, "since we know they're headed to the mountains."

"Eric and I are on our way," she says. "We'll pick you up in about ten minutes."

Nineteen

Hey, Samantha," says Eric, as I hop into the backseat of their unmarked car. As usual, he is casually dressed and looks like a regular guy, like he could be one of my brother's friends. I doubt most people would ever suspect he's a cop. "How's it going?" he asks.

"I'm not sure," I admit. "But it's great to see you guys."

"Samantha's been busy," Ebony says. "She's been doing some impressive undercover investigating for us."

"And it's been lonely," I say.

Eric laughs. "That's why most cops have partners. You need some backup in our line of work, Samantha."

I explain how I usually involve Olivia, but because this task force was top secret, I couldn't tell her a thing.

"We've made some real progress these past couple of weeks," says Ebony. "A few more arrests, and things might actually slow down a bit."

"That's Tate's apartment up there," I point out the window. "The one on the corner, second floor."

"Looks dark in there," observes Eric.

He parks near the stairway that's closest to apartment 214 and leads the way up the stairs. Then he knocks on the door, announcing, "Police, open up," and waits about a minute before he pulls out his crowbar and forces the door open. "Police," he says again. "We're coming in."

It's dark in the apartment, but Ebony finds a light and turns it on. The place, not surprisingly, is very messy. Clothes are strewn about. There are dirty dishes and carry-out boxes as well as a slew of empty booze bottles all over the place. My guess is that these boys have been partying hearty just about 24/7.

"There's the lovely red sofa," I say as I point to the back of a worn-out piece of furniture. There are dark stains and a large rip that exposes some white stuffing in the back. Eric walks around to the other side and suddenly stops. I can tell by his expression that something is wrong.

I freeze, and Ebony steps in front of me, her gun ready for backup. I suddenly wonder if I'm wrong. What if Zach and Tate are still here? Maybe they decided to wait until—

"You don't need your gun," he tells Ebony as he kneels beside the sofa.

We both hurry over to join him, and there is Felicity—face pale, eyes closed, with one hand over her mouth, the other one twisted behind her back, exactly like my dream. Even the syringe is there. My legs begin to shake, and my head is starting to spin. "Is she dead?" I whisper, but I think I know the answer.

Ebony puts an arm around me and guides me out of the apartment. "Sit down," she commands when we get to the stairs.

I don't argue. My rubbery legs give way, and I sit down on the top step, hanging my head between my knees as I begin to sob. "Oh, God," I cry, "Oh, God…why?"

I can hear Ebony on the phone, explaining the situation and asking them to send backup and the medical examiner. Finally she hangs up and puts her hand on my shoulder. "You okay?"

I look up at her. "Not really."

"I know this is hard, Samantha. Probably the hardest thing about being a cop. And trust me, it never gets any easier. That's the truth."

"I feel like it's my fault."

"No." She sits down beside me and cups my chin in her hand, forcing me to look into her face. "It is not your fault. If anything, you did all you could to warn this girl. You warned her boyfriend. You actually told her your vision, Samantha. It's not your fault. Do you understand?"

Tears are still streaming down my cheeks, and I can't catch my breath. "I just—just feel—so—so horrible."

"I know you do. We all do. No one likes to see this sort of thing happen. It's tragic."

"I wish we could've done something…something more."

"Short of having her locked up, which would've lasted about twenty-four hours, there was nothing you or anyone else could do. You need to accept that."

"But why?" I sob. "Why did God give me that vision…if I couldn't help her? I just don't get it."

"God has His reasons, Samantha. We don't always understand, but we have to trust Him. Maybe God just wanted to give Felicity another chance."

"But she wouldn't take it…"

"No, she wouldn't."

A police car with flashing blue lights is pulling into the parking lot now. "Come on," says Ebony, helping me to stand. "Let's get you downstairs and in the car. I need to go look around some more, collect some evidence."

I let her lead me to the car and help me into the front seat. "Will you be okay?" she asks as she locks the doors. I nod, although I seriously doubt this. I don't think I'll ever be completely okay again. I feel numb as I sit there. And confused. Why has this happened? What is the point? And why has God involved me? It all seems so pointless. So useless. Such a horrible waste. I lean forward, put my face in my hands, and continue to sob. *Why? Why? Why?*

I'm not sure how long I sit there crying, but finally the tears subside, and I look up to see there are a number of police cars around. There is yellow tape barricading the stairs, and people, probably neighbors, are nervously moving about the parking lot. I notice a cameraman sneaking under the yellow tape and creeping up the stairs. I guess the police will deal with him.

Someone taps on the passenger-side window, and I recognize the handsome face of Derrick Swanson from the six o'clock news. I can tell he wants to ask me a question. Probably something like, "Did you know Felicity Tompkins? Can you tell us how she died?"

I turn and look away, hiding my face with my hands in case someone tries to get me on film. Suddenly that image flashes through my mind again. That dead girl with a long strand of bright blue hair across her pale cheek. Poor Felicity. Why did she go back there? Why didn't she believe me? I wonder if Zach was involved, and yet I don't see how he could not be. He was living there with Tate, wasn't he? Surely he was aware of this. But why would these two guys just nonchalantly head out to go snow-boarding with a dead girl lying there on the sofa? Are they that heartless, that callous, that cruel? I know that drugs change people, but I cannot imagine Zach, my brother, being that cold.

I wonder where Zach and Tate are right now. I look at the clock to see that it's close to eight. They might be at the cabin by now. Something could've already gone wrong. Zach, like Felicity, might be dead right now. I suppress the urge to scream. I feel so helpless…so hopeless…. What's the use?

"Dear God," I begin to pray out loud, "I do not under-stand what's going on tonight. It feels like everything is spinning out of control. Is this all because of drugs? Please, please help Zach. I know he's made some very bad choices. Some very stupid choices. But he needs You. He desperately needs You. Please help him, God. Protect him tonight. Keep him safe. Bring him home." I continue to pray, sort of rambling and probably mostly incoherent, although I think God understands incoherent.

I open my eyes in time to see a gurney being pushed past the car. Her body is wrapped in gray, a good color for death. They wheel her to a police van with the initials ME—I'm sure for "medical examiner"—on the side. It seems obvious that her cause of death is drugs, more specifically an overdose. But they will probably check for other things. I close my eyes and try not to think of what kinds of other things…or how they could possibly relate to Zach. And then I feel sick—seriously sick. I open the door, jump out of the car, bend over, and vomit on the asphalt. Again and again I heave, barely managing to stay on my feet because my head is so dizzy. I'm about to fall over when I feel a pair of hands on my shoulders, and Eric is helping me into the backseat.

Camera lights are flashing, and I hear Ebony yelling at someone, "You can't print those without permission! She's a minor, and her parents can and probably will sue you."

"Let's get out of here," says Eric as he gets into the driver's seat. He turns on his flashing light, the one that's hidden inside the car, and then he hits a siren like a warning for spectators and newspeople to get out of the way.

"Keep your head down, Samantha," commands Ebony. "I don't trust those news folks any farther than I can throw them."

Once we're out of the parking lot, Eric turns off his flashing light. "Where are we going, ladies?"

"Do you want to go home now, Samantha?" asks Ebony.

"I don't know…," I mutter. Then I admit that my mom's not home and won't be until late.

"Why don't we take her back to the station with us?" says Eric.

"Yes," I say quickly. "Why don't you?"

Back at the station, Ebony checks her messages and makes some phone calls while Eric tries to cheer me up with some hot chocolate from the machine. Unfortunately, it tastes like cardboard. Or maybe it's just me.

"Samantha," says Ebony in a very serious tone. "I need to talk to you."

I look at her eyes and can tell that something is wrong. Very wrong.

"Come in my office."

Once I'm seated across from her, she sighs deeply,

and I think I can see her eyes getting moist. "What's wrong?" I ask. "Does it have to do with Felicity?"

"Tell me again what Zach was wearing in your dream…when you found him facedown in the snow."

"His Gap denim jacket and white Adidas tennis shoes," I say in a wooden voice that doesn't even sound like me.

"Right…" She picks up a pen and rolls it between her fingers.

"Why?"

"I heard back from the authorities, the ones at the ski resort where Zach and Tate were headed."

"And?"

"You were right about Chuck Denton's cabin. They tracked it down. And there had been a fire…and a shooting."

My hand flies up to my mouth. "Is it Zach?"

"The young man's pockets were empty. No ID. But he had on a denim jacket and a pair of white Adidas."

"Is he…is he…dead?"

Ebony gets up now and comes over to my side of the desk. She wraps her arms around me and begins to sob. "I'm so sorry, Samantha. So very, very sorry."

Things get very, very blurry now. I feel as if someone has just pulled the plug on my life. Maybe it's God. Maybe it's Satan. But something in me just dies…and I do not see how I can go on.

"Here," says Eric as he hands me a glass of water. I'm not sure how much time has passed, but both Eric and Ebony are looking at me with worried eyes.

"Are you okay?" asks Ebony.

"No."

"Yes. I would expect that." She's gently rubbing my back. I can tell she's doing this, but it's like I can't feel it. Like I can't feel anything.

"Do we need to take you to a doctor or anything?" asks Eric.

"No."

"I tried to call your mother," says Ebony, "but her phone's turned off, and I just couldn't leave a message. Not about something like this."

I look at the clock above Ebony's desk. It's 9:25. "They're at a concert in the city," I say in a flat tone. "She said it'll go until midnight."

Ebony frowns and looks at Eric.

"They need someone to identify the body, Samantha," he says in a quiet voice.

"I think it's too much for her," says Ebony.

"No," I say. "Let's go."

"Are you sure?"

But I'm already on my feet, opening the office door. Like a programmed robot, I'm going down the hallway, putting one foot in front of the other, pushing open the exit door that leads to the stairs to the garage. Soon we're back in Eric's car, I am slumped in the backseat again, and he is driving us through town. The city lights are blurry and fuzzy and weird. I'm not sure if it's from the rain or the tears. Everything about tonight seems surreal and impossible. And I actually begin to think I'm just having one of those dreams. I lean back, close my eyes, and surrender to it. I surrender to God. I figure if He's going to kill me anyway, since that's what this feels like, He might as well get on with it.

"Samantha," says Ebony. "We're here."

"Huh?" I open my eyes and then blink at the bright light that's streaming into the backseat of the car. "Where am I?"

Ebony reaches in to help me out. "Remember...we're up in the mountains...at the sheriff's department...to see about Zach."

To see about Zach, to see about Zach... Those words keep echoing through my mind as Ebony and Eric lead me into a small brick building. And then I remember. Oh yeah, Zach has been shot. He's dead. We need to identify him. I notice a clock as we go inside. It's eleven thirty. Mom and Steven are still at the concert. Hasn't it been about a week since they went up there? Shouldn't they be back by now?

"Right this way," says a man in a tan uniform. I think someone told me his name, but it went right over my head. I'm not really functioning at full capacity just now. I wonder if I'm really here at all.

It's a small room. Brightly lit. There is a table off to one side. Not an impressive table like you see on television shows. It looks more like the kind of folding table the church might use for a potluck. This is not a potluck. On top of the table is a body that's draped in a white tarp. Zach.

"Are you ready, miss?" asks the uniformed man.

"Ready?" I hear my voice ask. Ebony and Eric are both holding my hands, one on each side, almost as if they plan to catch me when I fall. And I know I will fall. My legs are already shaking.

"Go ahead," says Ebony. "Let's get this over with."

We're standing near the head now. The man carefully

peels back the cloth, just enough to expose the face. I stare and stare and I feel confused. Really confused. Then I turn and look at Ebony and Eric, as if I think they can help me.

"It's not him!" exclaims Ebony.

"It's not, is it?" I say.

"It's not." Ebony turns and looks at me with relief. "It's not Zach."

I reach out and hug her. "It's not Zach, Ebony! It's not him."

All three of us are hugging each other as the sheriff replaces the drape over the unfortunate young man's face. His hair, unlike Zach's, is dark, almost black.

"Sorry," Ebony tells the sheriff. "We can't help you."

"I don't suppose you know who the fella is, do you?" he asks me. "A friend of your brother's perhaps?"

"I've never seen him," I admit. "And it's not Tate."

He nods. "Sorry you made the trip up here for nothing."

I stare at him. "Oh, no, it wasn't for nothing. Don't you understand? My brother is alive."

He nods without commenting. I suppose he's thinking my brother may be alive but he's probably a criminal. Well, whatever. I'd rather see Zach alive and doing time... than dead.

Twenty

I feel like I'm slowly coming back to life as we drive toward town. I try my mom's cell phone again, but it's still turned off. Finally I decide to leave a message at our house, telling her why I'm not home. Well, not with all the gory details. I don't want her to freak.

"Where do you think Zach and Tate are now?" I ask Ebony.

"The sheriff said that Tate's uncle's cabin burned to the ground," she explains. "Just like in your dream."

"But the guy, the one who was shot in the back, wasn't he actually wearing a denim jacket and Adidas tennis shoes?"

"According to the sheriff."

"But lots of people wear denim jackets," points out Eric. "I have a couple myself. And Adidas are pretty common too."

"Common…but why was that exactly like my dream?" I persist, still trying to make sense of this puzzle. "And why was I so certain it was Zach?"

"But you never saw Zach's face, did you?"

"No," I admit. "I guess I just assumed it was him."

"I wonder who that guy really was," says Ebony. "Zach

and Tate didn't mention anyone else going snowboarding with them, did they?"

"No. But they weren't exactly forthcoming with information. In fact, Zach was getting pretty irritated with me. And Tate actually accused me of stalking him."

"Oh, my." Ebony sounds alarmed, and a chill runs down my spine. Am I in real danger?

"We've put out an APB on Tate's car," Eric says quickly. "We have the description and license, and if that vehicle is spotted, they will be picked up."

"And the apartment is under surveillance," adds Ebony. "As soon as we heard about Tate and Zach's incident in the mountains, we got the cops and everyone out of the apartment. Our guess is they're fleeing the burned cabin scene. And it seems only logical that they'll return to the apartment. At least long enough to get their things."

"And will they be arrested?" I ask.

"Yes, they'll definitely be detained for questioning," says Ebony. "And it's fairly certain that charges will follow."

"What if Zach decides not to go to the apartment?" I say suddenly. "What if he tries to come home?" I imagine my mom alone in our house and clueless.

"Good thinking. I'll put your house under surveillance too," says Ebony as she opens her phone. "For your protection and your mom's."

I listen as she makes the call. It's weird to hear her giving our home address, then giving Zach's and Tate's names and the description of Tate's car. It's like our little world has tilted sideways, and everything has become strangely skewed.

It's nearly two in the morning when we finally pull into my driveway. Mom's car is there, and the house lights are on, both inside and out. I'm guessing that Mom's still up. I hope my message wasn't too upsetting.

"That's the surveillance vehicle," says Ebony, pointing to what looks like a plumber's van parked one house down and across the street.

Eric hops out of the car, opens my door, and then escorts me up to the house. "You were really brave tonight, Samantha," he says as I fish out my house key to unlock the door.

"Thanks," I tell him. "I think it was the hardest night of my life."

"I'm glad it wasn't Zach."

"Hopefully, he's okay," I say as I insert the key, but before it even turns, Mom opens the door.

"Thank goodness," she says, pulling me into the house. "Now tell me exactly what is going on."

"Thanks, Eric," I say as he nods to both of us, telling us to take care.

It takes nearly an hour to tell Mom the whole story. We're up in her room, which feels safer somehow, sitting on her bed, and I am sparing no details. There's no point in protecting Zach anymore. He's already in way over his head. Still, I can tell that she's totally shocked by this news. All color is drained from her face, and her hand is pressed tightly over her mouth.

"I know this all seems unbelievable," I say to her. "Just hearing myself tell you about this feels more like I'm relaying one of my dreams than what actually happened tonight. It's all been pretty surreal."

She just shakes her head, still speechless. But now streams of tears are running down her cheeks.

"I don't know what's going to happen to Zach, Mom, but I think we need to be prepared for the worst. At least he's not dead. At least not that we know."

She finally speaks. "I just can't believe all you've been through tonight, Samantha. And to think I didn't have a clue. Here Steven and I were off at this silly rock concert, acting like teenagers, and you were back here going through all—all of this." She begins to sob loudly now. "I'm so sorry, Sam. So sorry. I'm—I'm a horrible mother."

I lean over and hug her now. "No, you're not, Mom."

"I am," she protests. "I leave you home alone to deal with things—things like this—and Zach is out there doing God only knows what. I really am a terrible mom."

"You're a single mom doing the best you can," I say, "but you're doing it on your own, Mom. You really need God to help you. I can't imagine how you can carry that kind of load without God's help."

She sort of nods. "You know, I'm starting to wonder about that myself."

"When they told me Zach was dead…" I pause to study her face. "I thought about you, Mom. I thought, this is going to kill her too. First I lose Dad. Then Zach. And maybe you. I just felt so hopeless. So totally hopeless."

"And yet you still believed in God?" she asks. "In the midst of that hopelessness, you still believed in a God who could do something like that?"

"God was all I had in that moment. I was totally con-fused and scared, but I *knew* that God was there with me. I mean, it felt like all that pain was about to kill me.

I even wondered if God *wanted* to kill me. But despite everything, I knew He was there with me. I knew He wasn't going to leave me. He was my only lifeline, and I didn't let go."

The room gets quiet for a while, and I can tell she's mulling this over. I also know I could go on and on about God and how much we all need Him. But I think maybe less is more.

"So…what do you think is going to happen with Zach?" Mom finally asks.

"I don't know… It doesn't look good. But at least that wasn't him." I shudder. "When I saw that other guy…the second dead person I saw tonight…well, it was just so sad. So final."

"But it wasn't Zach."

"Zach is definitely in trouble," I tell her. "But I think Tate is in way more trouble. I mean, since it was his apartment where Felicity died…and his uncle's cabin where that guy was murdered."

"Do you think Zach and Tate were involved in that murder?"

"I just don't know, Mom."

"There wasn't anything about that in your dream?"

I shake my head. "My dreams and visions are more like quick glimpses. Kind of like having a couple of pieces to a big puzzle."

"Important pieces."

I'm surprised to hear her say this. She's usually down on my "gift." Maybe something is changing in her.

"Well, it's really late, Samantha. You must be exhausted. Will you be able to sleep?"

I consider this. "I don't know…"

"Why don't you just stay in here for the night?" she suggests. "It's only a few hours until morning anyway."

I sigh gratefully. "Thanks, Mom."

"I'm glad that surveillance van is down there," she says after turning out the light. "I feel a little safer."

"Me too." But the truth is, I still have some extremely frightening images in my head. The only thing that makes me truly feel safe is knowing that God is here with us. I imagine myself sleeping in the palm of His hand.

The next morning we awake to the sound of the phone ringing. It's early, not even seven. I feel certain this call is about Zach. I sit up, fully alert and bracing myself for the worst, as Mom answers.

"Oh…," she says with a deeply creased brow. "But he's okay?" She listens for a while, then finally says, "Yes, we'll come." Then she hangs up and looks at me. "That was Ebony. They picked up Zach a few hours ago."

I nod. "And?"

"That's about all I know. He's been questioned, but they haven't charged him with anything too serious…yet."

"Are they releasing him?"

"Ebony said that's not been determined yet." Mom looks confused now. "They may set bail, and if I post it, they release him to my custody."

"Don't do it, Mom," I say suddenly. *"Do not do it."*

"Really?"

"Yes. You know I love Zach. You know I want what's best for him. But I honestly think he's safer in jail for now."

She considers this. "You're probably right."

So we get dressed, grab a quick bite to eat, then

head downtown where Ebony and Eric are waiting for us in her office.

"He's told us a few things," Eric begins, "and he *acts* like he wants to cooperate."

"But he's also trying to make it very clear that he wasn't totally aware of Tate's dealings," adds Ebony.

"Tate's dealings?" echoes my mom.

"We know that Tate has been working with his uncle, distributing meth around the state," says Ebony.

"It's quite an operation," adds Eric. "The automotive-parts business provided a nice little cover. But with Samantha's findings and some other evidence, we're shutting them down for good."

"Chuck Denton, the uncle, is in police custody at this time." Ebony glances at me. "And I'm sure he's not too thrilled to learn that his cabin got torched last night."

"Tate is still on the run," says Eric. "And we suspect he may have a serious load of meth on him—as well as cash."

"Does Zach know where Tate is?" I ask.

"He says he doesn't." Ebony frowns. "But I'm not sure. He's being pretty tight-lipped when it comes to his buddy."

"Does Zach know about Felicity?" I ask.

"He does now," says Eric. "He actually seemed pretty shocked."

"What did he say?"

"He said they'd been partying with her. She'd spent a couple of nights at the apartment. But he swears she was fine when they left yesterday. He said she was 'sleeping it off.'"

"Permanently sleeping it off," I say in a slightly angry tone.

Eric nods with understanding. "But he did seem genuinely sad about it, Samantha. I don't think that was an act."

"What about the dead guy we saw last night?" I persist. "Did Zach know anything about him?"

"He said he didn't know a thing, never heard of the guy, never saw him," says Ebony. "But I still get the feeling he's holding back."

I consider this. I'm almost certain that the guy had on Zach's jacket and shoes. Oh, I never saw them on him for real, but in that dream...it seemed so real. "Would it be okay if I talk to Zach alone?" I ask. "I mean, *after* Mom goes in, of course."

"That's okay," Mom says quickly. "You can talk to him first. It doesn't matter one way or another to me. I don't know what I'll say to him anyway. Right now I'm feeling so enraged at my son's behavior that I'm afraid I'll go in there and tear his head off."

"That probably won't help him to open up much," I say.

Ebony smiles. "Maybe you ladies can play good cop/bad cop. Samantha, you can start out as good cop."

"Works for me," says Mom.

"I can take you down there, Samantha," offers Eric, "if you're ready."

I take a deep breath. "As ready as I'll ever be."

Mom turns to Ebony. "Know where I can get a cup of coffee around here?"

"Of course."

"I think you might be able to get through to him," Eric tells me as he walks me down a hallway. "Any information you can extract will be much appreciated. We need to get our hands on Tate. The sooner the better."

"I'd like to get my hands on Tate too," I say.

Eric sort of laughs. "Leave that to the law. By the way, the room is wired so we can listen. Zach knows all about this and has signed a waiver, but he's so tired he may have forgotten. And that's okay. We need him to relax and loosen up. Remember, the most important thing is to get him to talk about Tate. But you probably shouldn't start there."

"I'll do what I can."

We stand in front of a door next to a big window that I suspect is one-way glass since Zach is sitting there on the other side just staring at it with the blankest look on his face. He's wearing a bright orange jumpsuit, which makes his pale, unshaven face look ghostly. He's got dark shadows beneath his eyes, and I notice he has several red spots, which I suspect are lesions from meth. So much for his "I'm clean" claims. But I don't want to go there right now. My brother looks like he's been to hell and back. He has a bruise on his cheek, and his hair is dirty and messy. But it's the expression in his eyes that worries me. It's the look of complete and utter hopelessness. Like he thinks he's going to rot in jail. Maybe he is.

"How long do I have with him?" I ask.

"As long as you need."

"Okay." I nod toward the door. "I'm ready." Of course, that's ridiculous. How can I possibly be ready? But I am praying silently as I walk in. Zach looks up and seems a tiny bit relieved that it's me. But then he scowls like he's not.

"What're you doing here?" he growls at me.

"I just came to talk, Zach."

"Everyone wants to talk."

"Actually, I'm hoping I can help you. But I can only help you if you're willing to tell me the truth. Anything else and I'm outta here, okay?"

He holds up his hands, which are cuffed together. "Are you calling me a liar?"

"You're not a liar, Zach. But drugs make people lie. And they make people do strange things they might not do otherwise."

He sort of nods.

"You've put Mom and me through a lot lately. You have no idea."

"Well, I've been through a lot too, Sis. You think this is fun?"

"No, but your choices got you here. Mom and I get dragged along because we're your family...because we still love you, Zach."

"Yeah, well, I'm sorry. I wish you didn't have to see me like this."

"The only reason I'm here is because I really care about you, and I want you to get a fair shake. Most of all, I want to see the truth come to light." I pause, wondering where to go next. Then it hits me. "You know, I saw a friend of mine last night. A girl I cared about and had been trying to help. I saw Felicity on...on Tate's couch." My voice cracks. "That was a really hard thing to see."

"I already told them that I didn't know she was dead. Honest. The last time I saw her, she was fine."

"I heard that you told them she was 'sleeping it off.' Just what does that mean? She was fine, but she was unconscious?"

"She had been fine, Sam. Then she fell asleep."

I remember the syringe. "Had she been shooting up?"

"I don't know…"

"Come on, Zach. You do too know."

"A bunch of people were there the night before. Everyone was doing something to get high." Then he stops. "Well, everyone but Tate. He doesn't do the hard stuff."

I narrow my eyes. "I find that hard to believe."

"Then don't. But you asked for the truth."

"Okay, explain it to me, Zach. Why would Tate have that stuff if he's not using?"

"'Cause he's smarter than me?"

"You mean because he sells that crud to make money?"

"I never really saw him sell it, Samantha. That's the truth."

"So he just gives it away?"

"Yeah. He's given it to me."

I suppress the urge to scream. Is my brother so stupid that he thinks free meth is a *gift*? "So did you ever see Tate pick anything up? Deliver anything? Were you ever with him on these runs? And you might as well know that I've seen you with him at Chuck's store."

"I thought he worked there."

"Apparently he *did* work there. He was his uncle's delivery boy. You were his helper. But you guys weren't delivering nuts and bolts and carburetors. You really didn't know that?"

"Look, Sam, hindsight is twenty-twenty. Sure, now I can see that Tate was probably grooming me to be his helper. I'm not totally stupid. People don't give you meth for free. They want something in return."

"What did Tate get in return from Felicity?"

"What do you think?"

"Sex?"

Zach nods, but his gaze is downward.

"How about you, Zach? Did you get to participate in that too?" Okay, I totally hate asking him this, but I'm certain the ME has taken DNA samples that could incriminate Zach if he was involved with Felicity like that. Might as well get it out in the open.

He glares at me now. "Not that it's any of your business, but no. I'm not like that. Besides, she was Tate's girl." Suddenly he gets this look in his eye, like he's just remembered something.

"What is it?" I ask. "Something about Felicity? You should know that she told me a few things too."

"Yeah," he says. "Come to think of it, she was telling Tate about how you and she had been talking. She was asking him how you knew about his red couch. She thought you'd been to the apartment. And for some reason this made Tate really mad. He already didn't trust you. But after Felicity said that, he was pretty mad at her. He told her not to talk to you, said you were a narc."

"When?" I ask. "When did he say those things?"

Zach runs his fingers through his matted hair with a confused expression. "I don't know. Friday morning, I think. Was it just yesterday?"

"Before Felicity took her little nap?"

"Yeah, I guess so. I really wasn't paying much attention. And then I took a long shower. When I got out, she was asleep on the couch."

"Asleep or OD'd?"

"I don't know."

"But you think it's possible, don't you?"

He doesn't say anything, just looks down at the table.

"Look, Zach," I say firmly. "I'm only here to help *you*. I think Tate's done some really bad things…and you're being dragged into them. You have to speak up, you have to tell the truth, or you may get blamed right along with him."

"I know…but I was high, Sam. I wasn't thinking straight. My head is still pretty fuzzy."

"Okay, then think back to last night. You guys were going snowboarding, right? Did you ever actually make it to Uncle Chuck's cabin?"

He slowly nods.

"Was there anyone with you?"

He doesn't answer.

"You know who I mean—the guy who got shot last night. Who was he, Zach?"

He still doesn't answer. Okay, this worries me. It convinces me that Zach really was involved. He seems to know something, something he won't say. I shoot up a silent prayer, and that's when I know I should tell him about my dream. I take him through the whole thing, complete with explicit details. He just listens, and I'm not sure whether he believes me or not.

"And if you think I'm making it up, I can prove it," I say finally. "I made notes of it last week, and Ebony knew about it before the shooting ever occurred."

"You really dreamed that?" He looks fairly stunned, and I think I have his attention.

"Yes. I honestly thought the guy in the dream was you. I was so worried that you were going to die, Zach. I mean, I could've sworn that was your denim Gap jacket and your white Adidas."

"They were."

"What do you mean, 'they were'?"

"The guy was wearing my jacket and my shoes."

"Why?"

"He was at the cabin when we got there. Waiting outside and shivering in the cold. He'd hiked in, just like we did. I had no idea who he was, but Tate seemed to be expecting him. I think his name was something Hispanic like Fernando or Hernando. I'm not sure. But he didn't have on weatherproof things, and he hadn't brought any extra clothes or boots with him. It was freezing cold up there, and his flimsy shoes were soaking wet, and he didn't even have a jacket. So I loaned him some of my stuff. The Gap jacket wasn't that warm, but I wasn't about to give him my parka. And my Adidas were too big, but he didn't seem to mind since they were dry."

"Really?" I lean over, fascinated. "Then what?"

"I thought we were going to get something to eat. But then Tate and this dude started getting into this big argument. I don't even know what it was about. I'd been trying to make a fire 'cause it was freezing in there, but the wood was wet, and it wasn't working. Anyway, I was starving and cranky and just wanted to go find some food. I'd been high all day, and it makes you hungry."

"Tell me about the fight. What happened next?"

"They started really going at each other. I thought someone was going to get seriously hurt." He shakes his head like he wishes he could shake the memory away. "Naturally, I jump in and try to help Tate, my buddy. So now all three of us are going at it, and we crash around the cabin until we knock over a table with a kerosene lantern going…'cause there's no electricity up there."

"A fire…just like in my dream."

"Yeah…" Zach stares at me funny again. "So the next thing I know, the whole place is on fire. I run outside and tell them to get out too, but they're still in there fighting like they both want to go up in flames."

"And?"

"My memory is kind of fuzzy. I think I was sort of shocked by everything. I mean, I thought we went up there to have a good time, and now there's a fight, and the cabin is going up in flames. So I'm standing outside yelling at them to get outta there, and pretty soon they both come walking out, just as calm as you please. The fire's going pretty good, and I see flames leaping behind them, and I'm relieved they're out. I thought for sure they were both gonna be toast. So Tate's walking behind this other dude, and they get a ways from the house, and then—*kabam!* I hear this loud blast, and the Hispanic dude falls facedown in the snow."

"He'd been shot?"

Zach nods with wide eyes. "Man, I just couldn't believe it, Sam. Tate had a gun, and he actually shot that guy. In the back!"

"Why wouldn't you tell the police this?" I ask.

"Tate swore he'd kill me if I did. He also said I'd be

partially to blame. He said I was an accessory to the crime, and we'd both go down."

"What happened next?"

"We hiked back to his car, threw our stuff in the trunk, and drove back to town. Neither one of us hardly spoke."

"But *you* got picked up, Zach. He didn't."

"Well, I had time to think about everything as we drove back. I knew it was crazy to stay with this guy. He was nuts. So we were barely in town, and he stopped to get gas. I said I had to use the john and then took off. I hid in a ditch for a long time. I think I actually fell asleep. I guess it was about four in the morning when I went back to the road and hitched."

"And got a ride with a cop?"

"Pretty much."

"Well, that cop was an angel in disguise."

His head is hanging now. "I'm in deep—"

"Not as deep as Tate."

"They'll never find him."

"How can you know that?"

"He's smart, Sam. He's always got a plan. And he's got money. Man, has he got money."

"Still, he could slip up."

Zach lays his head on the table now. "I am so sleepy, Sam. I just need a little nap. Okay?"

I reach over and put my hand on his messy hair. "Yeah. I understand. I'll be back later."

I turn and look toward the mirrored window and wave, curious as to whether anyone is really there. Within seconds the door opens, a uniformed officer comes in, and I go out.

"Way to go, Samantha," says Eric. "That was awesome."

"But we have to find Tate," I say urgently.

"Yeah. Maybe Zach can help us with that too."

"Maybe," I say. "Right now I think he just needs a nap." I blink and suppress a yawn. "I think I do too."

"Why don't you and your mom head for home?" he says. "Catch some z's. We'll let Zach get some rest too and some lunch. Then come back this afternoon and finish your interrogation."

I feel slightly indignant. "It's *not* an interrogation."

He smiles. "I know. But it's bringing the truth to light."

Twenty-One

Okay, just when a girl could really use some rest, I have another dream. And it turns out to be a rerun. I sit up in bed and try to recover from the horror of feeling like I'm about to burn to death, and then I realize—it's the exact same dream. The one I had several weeks ago with the windows that had canvas cloth nailed over them. Where could that place possibly be? And why am I having the dream again? It must be linked to Tate.

Mom's still asleep. I speak to her, but she's really out of it. So I write a note, set it on her pillow, and head back to the police station. I call Ebony as I wait for a stoplight.

"I had a dream," I say urgently. "I'm on my way back to the station now, and I need to talk to Zach."

"We'll have him ready."

Then I hang up, and as I drive, I pray. "God, I think You gave me that dream again for a reason. And I think it has to do with Tate. Maybe he's the guy who's trapped in the burning building. But the truth is, I don't really care if it is him. Part of me would like to see that monster go up in flames. But I know You are merciful, and maybe You have a reason to spare him. Please help us figure this out. Help Zach remember anything that could be useful. Amen."

Ebony meets me at the front door and walks me back to the "interrogation" room where Zach is waiting.

"Did you have a nap?" I ask. He still looks pretty sleepy.

"Not a very long one."

"Me neither. But that's because I had another dream."

He perks up slightly.

"I think it has to do with Tate, and I'm hoping you can help me with it, Zach."

"Go for it."

So I tell him all the details I can remember about this place. The canvas-covered windows, the location that I think was on an alley, the lampposts. He listens with interest, but he seems kind of blank.

"Come on," I urge him. "Think about it. Did Tate ever take you to a place like that?"

"He took me to a lot of places. I thought we were delivering auto parts." He laughs. "Man, am I a sucker." He shakes his head. "Tate must've seen that word stamped right across my forehead. This dude is straight out of rehab, and he is one great big *sucker.*"

I shut my eyes and let out a long sigh. "Oh man...you know I feel like that was my fault. I mean, I sort of brought Tate back into your life. He seemed so nice. So together. I remember how I stood there in the grocery store and told him about you coming home from rehab, and he sounded so concerned. I can't believe I invited him to our house." I clench my fists. "It was like inviting the devil to dinner. I'm so sorry, Zach."

He looks up at me and smiles. "Hey, you can't blame yourself, Sis. I probably would've run into him sooner or later. Brighton's not that big. Besides, it's like they say in rehab. Drugs are everywhere. It's up to us to walk away. And I didn't." Just then he slaps his forehead. "Hey, did you say something about the curtains being nailed to the wall?"

"Yes!"

"There was this place—it was kind of weird—over in the industrial part of town. It was really dark, and I do remember the curtains being nailed down. I asked the dude about it, and he said it was his darkroom. He didn't just work on cars and stuff, but he used the space to develop photos too. I remember thinking that probably explained the smell. But now I'm pretty sure he used that space to cook meth. See, I really am a big fat sucker, Sam. Your big brother is a first-rate idiot."

"Can you remember where that place was specifically?" I persist. He scratches his head, and before long, he narrows it down to several streets in the industrial area.

"I think it was two story, and the building had bricks on the outside," he adds. "The kind that have been painted a few times too many. And a big gray metal door that looked new, probably to keep people out."

"Good," I tell him. "That should help." I stand up now. "I guess you can finish your nap if you want."

He yawns.

"I think Mom will be in later."

He rolls his eyes. "Can't wait for that show to begin."

"And just so you know, Zach, she won't be bailing you out anytime soon. We both think you need to just chill for a while."

He shrugs. "Don't know that I really care, little sister. I'm thinking this is a pretty cheap rehab program."

I smile at him. "Yeah, but it's all up to you whether it works or not, isn't it?"

"That's right."

Ebony and Eric are both in the hallway when I go out. Both of them are smiling.

"Way to go," says Eric.

"I already sent out the description of the building," Ebony tells me. "People are looking for it right now."

"Good." I suppress a yawn.

"You didn't have much of a nap. Why don't you go home and get some rest now?" says Ebony.

"Your mom just got here," says Eric. "She says she's ready to talk to Zach without ripping his head off now."

"A real nap does sound good," I admit. "But you guys must be just as tired as I am. When do you get a rest?"

"Hopefully we'll all rest easy after this is wrapped up," says Eric. "I'll sleep easier when I know that Tate Mitchell is off the streets."

"I just hope you get him soon," I say. "I mean, it seemed pretty dicey in my dream. There's the part about breaking through the window… I'd hate to think he could get away after that." Suddenly I remember something. I glance at my watch to see that it's one twenty in the afternoon. "But wait," I say. "In my dream it all seemed to go down at night. It's too early!"

Ebony pulls out her cell phone. "I'll tell our guys to hold off." She calls the dispatcher and explains the situation. "Make it very clear," she says carefully. "If they find the place, they are not to go in. Do not stick around. We'll set up a surveillance van. It's likely the suspect is not even there yet. We do not want to jump in too soon. Is that clear?" Then she hangs up.

"That could've really messed things up," says Eric.

"Yes." Ebony nods. "What a tip-off if Tate shows up and sees cop cars crawling all over the place."

"We're guessing he's switched vehicles by now," says Eric.

"Yes, he won't make this easy."

"I can't say for sure," I tell them, "but in my dream, it seemed like it was pretty late at night since the streets were very quiet. No traffic or anything."

"The industrial district usually is pretty quiet after dark," Eric tells me. "So it might've been earlier."

"Whenever it is, we'll be there," says Ebony. "Go ahead and take off if you want, Samantha. I think your work here is done. At least for now."

Eric slaps me on the back. "You really are amazing, girl."

"It's God, not me," I say. "But thanks anyway."

When I get home, I'm tired but not sleepy. And I really want to talk to someone. It's Saturday, and Conrad and his family are on their way to Disneyland. And I suspect that Olivia and her family are probably on their way to Seattle now since their cruise ship leaves tomorrow morning, but I decide to try her cell anyway. She'll be out of range once they're on the ship. Her phone must be off, because I go straight to her messaging. Even so, it's comforting to hear her voice. "Hi, Olivia," I say. "This is Sam. I hope you have a great time on your cruise. We'll have a lot to talk about when you get back. Love you!"

I considered saying more, but it would take so much explaining to really cover the last twenty-four hours of my life. I sit down at the table and pick up the newspaper. Of course, there's the dreaded headline: Teen Girl Dies of Overdose. They don't disclose her name "until all family members are notified," but they do give the address of the apartment building. And suddenly I think of Jack. Poor Jack. I have no idea what his cell number is, but it occurs to me that his old band friend, Cameron, should know. And I think I have Cameron's number since he's called me before to reach Olivia. I go back into my cell phone's history, and there it is: Cameron Vincent. I press Send and wait to see if he answers. It's possible that he's off on some wild spring-break vacation too. That wouldn't surprise me. But then he answers.

"Hey, Cameron," I say. "This is Samantha."

"What's up?"

I sigh. "A lot, actually… Anyway, it probably seems weird, but I'm looking for Jack McAllister's cell-phone number. Do you have it?"

"Sure." He shoots off the numbers. "But why?"

"Did you see the newspaper…about the teen who died of an overdose?"

"No. Why?"

"That was Felicity Tompkins."

"No way."

"Yeah."

"Man, that's terrible. Felicity was cool. I can't believe she's dead."

"I know. I feel really bad too. And I know Jack's going to be crushed. He really cared about her."

"Was he to blame at all? I mean, was he involved in the drug part of it with her?"

"No," I say quickly. "Not at all. In fact, you might be interested to know that Jack doesn't do the hard stuff. He never has. He was worried about Felicity and what she was doing."

"You know, I didn't think he was into it that much. But even so, he was pretty stupid to get caught smoking weed at my house."

"It seems like a double standard," I say. "I mean, according to Olivia, you guys indulge in it too sometimes—although she told me that you don't do it when she's around. Anyway, it hurt Jack a lot to be let go from the band like that."

"I can't believe you're taking his side."

"Jack's a nice guy. I mean, he puts on a tough-guy front, but he's been through a lot."

"I know…"

"And he's about to go through a lot more, Cameron. He needs some friends right now."

"Yeah, I guess so…" He sighs loudly. "So you think it was a mistake for me to kick him out?"

"I think you should talk to him about it."

"And what about Olivia? She's the one who drew the line, and I kinda think she's right."

"I do too. But I also think you need to talk to Jack. Whether you ask him back into the band or not is up to you. I mean, you could make it clear that you won't tolerate any substance abuse during practices or gigs. But at least give the guy a chance to respond. I think he might be changing, especially after this thing with Felicity."

"Yeah, that's really tough. Are you going to call him now?"

"That's my plan."

"Will you call me back and tell me how he's doing, like whether I should call him today or not?"

"Sure," I tell him. "No problem."

I hang up and call Jack, and when he answers, I can tell by his voice that he knows.

"This is Samantha," I say. "And I'm guessing you've heard the news."

He cusses, and I don't really blame him.

"I just wanted to call and say how sorry I am, Jack. The whole thing just makes me sick."

"Yeah, me too."

"And if you need to talk…well, I'm here."

"How do you know about it?" he asks. "The papers didn't print her name or anything."

"It's a long story, Jack."

"I'd like to hear it."

"Want to meet at Lava Java?" I ask.

"I'm on my way."

"See ya."

I call Cameron back and tell him I'm going to meet Jack at Lava Java. "He sounds pretty depressed," I say.

"Yeah, the more I think about it, the worse I feel. That guy just didn't need something like this in his life. He's been through enough."

"I know."

"Tell him I want to talk to him. Maybe he can give me a call after you guys have coffee."

"Sure."

Jack is already there when I arrive. He looks seriously bummed. And why wouldn't he be? I get a coffee and go over and sit down across from him. "Hey."

"Hey."

I take a deep breath and begin my story. I've decided not to tell him everything I know, but I do tell him about Zach being in jail and that we think Tate Mitchell could be to blame for Felicity's death.

"I'll kill him."

"I know how you feel, Jack." I take a sip of coffee. "I think I could've killed him myself last night. The guy is a total jerk."

Then Jack uses a few more colorful words to describe Tate Mitchell.

I just listen, waiting for him to cool down some. "Hopefully he'll get arrested and get what's coming to him."

Jack just shakes his head. "Life in prison? What's that compared to what he's done?"

"I know…"

"I want him to suffer. I want him to burn in hell. I want—"

"I know you're angry, Jack. I am too. But that's not going to change anything. It won't bring her back, and it'll only make you more miserable."

He looks at me with red eyes. He's been crying. "So, what then? What do I do?"

I sigh and shake my head. "All I can tell you is what I do, Jack. I have to lean hard on God in times like this. He is the only thing I have to hold on to that makes any sense." Then I tell him about how I thought my brother had been murdered last night. I tell about the drive up into the mountains to identify the body and how hopeless I felt.

Jack's listening like he understands.

"I mean, here I'd just found out about Felicity—and then I think my brother's dead too. It was overwhelming."

He nods. "But your brother was alive?"

"Yeah, but I didn't know that for a couple of hours. All I had then was God."

"Can I ask you something, Sam?"

"Sure."

"You said you were at the apartment yesterday, right?"

"Yeah. The police were looking for my brother and Tate, and they asked me to help."

"So, was it like your vision, the one you told Felicity about? Did she really die on a beat-up red couch?"

I just nod. "It was exactly like that." Then I start to cry, which surprises me because I thought I was surely out of tears by now. "I just wish she had listened to me, Jack. I just wish she had believed me. God was trying to warn her."

"I know…"

We talk for about an hour, and I know that Jack has a long way to go before he gets over this—if that's even possible. But I encourage him to give God a chance. "What's the worst that can happen?" I finally ask.

"He'll let me down."

"But you'll never know if you don't try Him first."

"Maybe…"

Then I tell Jack that Cameron wants to talk to him.

"You talked to Cameron?"

"I needed your number."

"Oh…"

Then we're outside, going to our cars, and I tell him I'll be praying for him and that he can call me if he needs to talk. "It might not seem like it, but you've got friends, Jack. You know that?"

He sort of nods, then wipes the edge of his eye with a fingertip. "See ya."

As I walk away, I hope that's true. I hope I'll be seeing more of this guy. I have a feeling God is up to something big in his life, and I'd like to remain involved.

Twenty-Two

The next morning I'm getting ready for church when my cell phone rings. It's Ebony, and she tells me she has news. I sit down on my bed and, barely breathing, wait for her to continue.

"We staked out the building last night. It fit the description perfectly. But there didn't appear to be anyone coming or going. Even so, we waited. Finally, about two in the morning, I was so exhausted that I went home. I figured we might have the wrong night. Of course the rest of the crew stuck around—just in case. Apparently, they noticed a light in the building around three. And then the light grew bigger and started to flicker, and they realized there was a fire going inside. They called the fire department, and because of the concern over hazardous materials due to the suspicion of a meth lab, they waited until the firefighters arrived. But before the firefighters could get in, there was an explosion, and a man literally exploded out the window, Samantha. Does this sound familiar?"

I nod without answering, then manage to whisper, "Yes."

"It was Tate Mitchell. He's under arrest but in the hospital being treated for third-degree burns, severe cuts and lacerations from the broken glass, involving hundreds of stitches, and, oh yes, poisoning from inhaling the toxic smoke, and most likely lung damage. He's one sick puppy."

"Is he going to live?"

"Oh, we feel very hopeful. He was upgraded from critical to serious this morning, and he was actually talking to the nurse. We asked the medical staff to do all they can to keep this man alive so we can take him to trial."

"I think his punishment has already begun," I say.

"I think it started a long time ago," says Ebony, "back when he first started playing with fire."

I didn't really think I had any big plans for spring break, but it turns out I was wrong. Ebony decides it's about time I have some serious training. As a result, I spend most of my week with her. It's like a cop crash course or Law Enforcement 101. Ebony and Eric teach me a lot about surveillance work, and Ebony even gives me several tests that turn out to be pretty fun. But if there's one thing she really drives home, it's that my safety is the force's number-one concern. And if I do anything foolish, anything that puts me in danger, I will be called on the carpet—and my "internship" will be history. I take this very seriously and promise to do my best.

Zach has a busy week too. Once he hears about Tate's arrest and condition (which is upgraded to fair), he decides it's safe to cooperate with the investigation. As a result, he spends a lot of time with the police and DA. By the end of the week, Ebony privately informs me that the DA may request a lockdown rehab treatment program in exchange for Zach's jail time. But it will be a long program.

Finally spring break and my training week come to an end. My friends are all back from their exciting (or in Alex's case, "excruciatingly boring") vacations, and on Monday morning we are all in school again. Naturally, everyone is shocked and saddened to hear about Felicity's death. And our school allows an early release for kids who want to attend her funeral service in the afternoon. I invite Jack to ride with me to the mortuary.

"I keep wondering what happens next," Jack says. We're on the way home from the cemetery, where we just watched Felicity's casket being lowered into the muddy ground. It's the first time he's spoken since the depressing service began more than two hours ago. Instead of having a pastor offer words of encouragement, Felicity's family allowed the funeral-home director to give her eulogy. Consequently, it was a fairly hopeless message.

"Next?" I adjust my windshield wipers. Today has been a mixture of drizzle, rain, and mist, very gray and gloomy.

"After we're dead. Like where is she really, Sam? I honestly don't think she's in that box that's six feet under right now. But is she in hell?"

I take in a sharp breath and consider my answer, but before I can say a thing, he speaks again. "She's not in heaven," he says quickly, "that's for sure."

"What makes you so sure?"

"She wasn't exactly a saint."

"No one is." Then I tell him about when Jesus was being crucified and those final words He said to the thief on the cross next to Him. "I'm sure no one expected that criminal to make it to heaven either. But when he accepted Jesus's forgiveness, he got his get-out-of-hell card for free."

"So are you saying that you know for sure Felicity is in heaven right now?" His voice drips with skepticism.

"I'm saying I don't know for sure that she's not." I let out a deep sigh as I slow down for a red light. "I think there will be a lot of surprises in heaven, Jack. And I'm saying God is a God of last chances. And He doesn't want anyone to go to hell.

"Oh…"

Now I don't claim to have all the answers—nobody does—but for some reason, I feel good about this one, like maybe God was helping me with it. And Jack seems to be seriously mulling it over as I drive him home.

"Thanks, Sam," he tells me when I pull up to his apartment complex. "For everything, you know."

"Thank you."

He frowns. "Why are you thanking me?"

"For being my friend."

Then he nods slightly. "Yeah…okay then…"

"See ya tomorrow," I call as he gets out of the car.

He waves. "See ya."

As I drive home, I feel a contrasting mixture of sadness and joy. I can't even explain it, but I think it's an emotion God is well acquainted with, and I feel honored that I can even experience it now.

As I park my car and walk toward the house, I notice the sun breaking through a slit in the clouds overhead. I look up to the sliver of golden light and am filled with an unexpected sense of hope. And suddenly I know that, despite the hard stuff in this life, God is right here with me, walking alongside and holding my hand.

————

With arms spread wide, the blonde steps back, staring down at her mint green formal gown now splattered with spots of bright red blood. When she looks up, her eyes widen in horror.

She sees her date, a dark-haired young man in a neat black tux, his face twisted in pain as his fists tighten and he crumples to the floor. He curls into a prenatal ball…and a dark, shiny pool of blood stains the clean white floor.

Music blares in the background, the bass thumping a fast beat. It's a Pretty Ricky song, but the only sound the pretty blonde can hear is coming from her boyfriend as he lets out a low growl followed by a gurgle. Then he jerks suddenly, convulsing, drawing a final gasping breath.

The girl bends over, reaches out her hand as if she wants to help him, and then, as though sensing danger, she stands and turns and desperately dashes in the opposite direction, tripping over her spiky high heels as she goes but continuing on…as if she is running for her life.

I wake up clinging to my comforter and still shaking. My heart pounds with a very real sense of fear, as if I, too, am in grave danger. It takes a long moment to realize that this was only a dream. Just a dream. But a very realistic and horribly tragic dream. Without turning on the bedside lamp, I reach for the notebook I keep handy for times like this, and in the gray dawn light, I take several deep calming breaths and begin to write.

I'm trying to capture all the still-vivid details—the style of the mint green gown (beaded with spaghetti straps, formfitting to the girl's good figure) and those metallic-toned shoes (bronze or gold?). I try to recall the girl's facial features (what made her so pretty?). I do recall what appeared to be diamond earrings, three piercings in one ear, smallest on top, largest on the bottom. (But was it only one ear? And if so, which ear was it? Right or left?) I close my eyes and try to see her again. Left. I believe it was left.

I remember the boy's hairstyle, short and neat as if he might be into sports. I try to describe his tux, but other than it being black, I draw a blank. I can't even remember his shoes, but I think they were black as well. I even write down a description of the floor as I remember it: large square tiles of white with streaks of gray throughout. Marble perhaps? I describe what the music sounded like (I don't even know why I think Pretty Ricky since I'm not a fan, but it's what went through my head). And then I remember strings of lights, glowing blurrily in the background. Like a party going on. (A wedding perhaps?)

I pause, searching my memory for more, trying to figure out if I've missed an important detail. Another person? A sound? A smell? Who had the gun? Or was the guy even killed with a gun? Perhaps it was a knife. I don't remember that part at all. Did I even see what happened? Is it possible that the girl was responsible? No, she seemed too shocked, too frightened. And yet, if she'd committed a crime, perhaps in the heat of the moment, it would make sense that she'd be shocked and scared. I make note of this too. But there must be more. Is there some little detail I missed? I shut my eyes again and just sit there in bed, trying to remember. But that seems to be it.

I close my notebook and set it back on the bedside table. I'll tell Ebony about this dream later today. I lie back down in bed, breathing deeply to calm myself. But who can sleep after a dream like that? I wish I could call Olivia and run it past her. I'm sure she'd have some thoughts. But it's not even six yet. Instead, I go to the kitchen and try to be quiet as I make coffee.

It must've been a prom, I decide as I pour water into the coffee maker. And that makes sense because it's spring, and already people are starting to pair off and plan for prom at my school. Even Olivia is starting to talk about it. She's pretty sure Alex is going to ask her. Naturally, she thinks Conrad will ask me as well. And I think it'd be fun to go to prom. That'd be a first for me, for sure. But what if there's going to be a murder that night? Still, I didn't recognize either of the people in my dream. And the girl, especially, had the kind of looks a person would remember. She looked like the kind of girl who would be well known.

Our prom is still a month away, so that gives me time. Unless it's not our prom. What if it's another school's prom? Who knows what dates that might include? I know that schools like to stagger the dates so the local restaurants aren't overwhelmed with all the high-school students going out to dinner before prom at the same time. It's possible another high school could have a prom as soon as next weekend. I will have to mention this to Ebony ASAP.

Reader's Guide

1. How did you feel when Zach first came home from drug rehab? Were you optimistic, like Sam, thinking that his life was on track again? Or did you have your doubts? Explain why.

2. When Sam suspected Zach was using again, she was reluctant to tell Ebony or her mom. What would you have done if you had been in the same position?

3. Why do you think Olivia labeled drug users as losers?

4. Tate came across as a great guy early in the story. How did you feel about him when you discovered his involvement in drugs?

5. What's your attitude toward kids who abuse substances like drugs or alcohol? Why do you feel the way you do?

6. How do you feel about addiction in general? How do you think God feels about addicts?

7. Jack asked Sam where Felicity went after death. Did you agree or disagree with what Sam told him? Why?

8. Why do you think Sam's mom still has some difficulty with Sam's unusual gift? What would you say to her?

9. Despite all the hard challenges that Sam faces, she manages to keep a fairly optimistic attitude. Why is that?

10. Where do you turn when life starts going sideways on you?

SO YOU WANT TO LEARN MORE
ABOUT VISIONS AND DREAMS?

As Christians, we all have the Holy Spirit within us, and God speaks through His Spirit to guide us in our walk with Him. Most often, He speaks through our circumstances, changing our desires, giving us insight into Scripture, bringing the right words to say when speaking, or having another Christian speak words we need to hear. Yet God, in His sovereignty, may still choose to speak to us in a supernatural way, such as visions and dreams.

Our dreams, if they are truly of the Lord, should clearly line up with the Word and thus correctly reveal His character. We must always be very careful to test the words, interpretations of circumstances, dreams, visions, and advice that we receive. Satan wants to deceive us, and he has deceived many Christians into thinking that God is speaking when He is not. So how do we know if it's actually God's voice we are hearing?

First we have to look at the Bible and see how and what He has said in the past, asking the question, *Does what I'm hearing line up with who God shows Himself to be and the way He works in Scripture?* Below is a list of references to dreams and visions in Scripture that will help you see what God has said about these gifts:

- Genesis is full of dreams and visions! Check out some key chapters: 15, 20, 28, 31, 37, 40, 41
- Deuteronomy 13:1–5

- Judges 7
- 1 Kings 3
- Jeremiah 23
- Several passages in the book of Daniel
- Joel 2
- The book of Ezekiel has a lot of visions
- There are a lot of dreams in the book of Matthew, specifically in chapters 1 and 2
- Acts 9, 10, 16, 18
- The whole book of Revelation

If you want to learn more and have a balanced perspective on all this stuff, you'll probably want to research the broader category of spiritual gifts. Every Christian has at least one spiritual gift, and they are important to learn about. Here is a list of books and Web sites that will help:

- *Hearing God's Voice* by Henry and Richard Blackaby
- *What's So Spiritual about Your Gifts?* by Henry and Mel Blackaby
- *Showing the Spirit* by D. A. Carson
- *The Gift of Prophecy in the New Testament and Today* by Wayne Grudem
- *Are Miraculous Gifts for Today?* by Wayne Grudem
- *Keep in Step with the Spirit* by J. I. Packer
- www.expository.org/spiritualgifts.htm
- www.enjoyinggodministries.com. Under the Theological Studies Section, choose Controversial Issues. Check out the third, fourth, and eighteenth sessions.

- www.desiringgod.org. Click on Resource Library and choose Topic Index. Then under Church & Ministry, check out Spiritual Gifts under Church Life.

(Note: If you're doing a Google search on spiritual gifts or dreams and visions, please make sure you type in *Christian* as well. This will help you weed out a lot of deceitful stuff.)

As you continue to research and learn about spiritual gifts, always remember: the bottom line is to focus on the Giver, not the gift. God gives to us so we can glorify Him.

Signs and wonders are not the saving word of grace; they are God's secondary testimony to the word of his grace. Signs and wonders do not save. They are not the power of God unto salvation. They do not transform the heart—any more than music or art or drama that accompany the gospel. Signs and wonders can be imitated by Satan (2 Thessalonians 2:9; Matthew 24:24), but the gospel is utterly contrary to his nature. What changes the heart and saves the soul is the self-authenticating glory of Christ seen in the message of the gospel (2 Corinthians 3:18–4:6).

But even if signs and wonders can't save the soul, they can, if God pleases, shatter the shell of disinterest; they can shatter the shell of cynicism; they can shatter the shell of false religion. Like every other good witness to the word of grace, they can help the fallen heart to fix its gaze on the gospel where the soul-saving, self-authenticating glory of

the Lord shines. Therefore the early church longed
for God to stretch forth his hand to heal, and that
signs and wonders be done in the name of Jesus.

—John Piper, *Desiring God*

It's a powerful gift with a lot of responsibility...

Bad Connection:

She seems like your average teen, but Samantha McGregor is unusually gifted. God gives her visions and dreams that offer unconventional glimpses into other people's lives and problems. In this first book in the Secret Life of Samantha McGregor series, Kayla Henderson is missing, and everyone, including Samantha, assumes she ran away. But then Samantha has a vision. If Kayla really is in danger, then time is running out!

Beyond Reach:

Garrett Pierson is one of those quiet, academic types. When Samantha, his chemistry partner, tries to draw him out, he shuts her down and requests a new partner. One day when Samantha prays for him, she has a vision of Garrett teetering on a railroad bridge—and then falling backwards, just beyond reach! What does this vision mean, and...where is Garrett, anyway?

Look for *Payback* Releasing in Spring 2008!

Available in bookstores and from online retailers.

MULTNOMAH BOOKS
www.mpbooks.com

Girl's Best Friend

ON MY OWN
Caitlin book four

I DO
Caitlin book five

JUST ASK.
Kim book one

MEANT TO BE
Kim book two

FALLING UP
Kim book three

THAT WAS THEN
Kim book four

In a diary format, this series captures the thoughts, emotions, and experiences of three very different teenage girls. Caitlin is a very sweet, strong Christian who's taken a non-dating stance; Chloe is a rock musician who's an extreme teen for Christ; and Kim is a Korean adoptee who's pursuing an authentic faith.

Join Maddie Chase
on all of her international adventures!

Now available in bookstores and from online retailers.

Faced with her son's crystal meth addiction and her husband's affair, Glennis Harmon searches for the ways she can best reach and help those she deeply loves.

Real-life struggles. A family's pain.
A hope for healing.

Bright and ambitious, college student Alice Laxton is diagnosed with schizophrenia—and embarks on a painful and eye-opening journey toward recovery and healing.